Changing the Narrative

Short Stories to Advance Everyday
Antiracism

Mark L. Joseph

Library of Congress Control Number: 2025920820

Paperback ISBN 979-8-9932780-0-1
eBook ISBN 979-8-9932780-2-5

Cover design by Joni Hirsch Kaden

For those who persevered and created
So that we can create and persevere

Kindness eases change.
Love quiets fear.
And a sweet and powerful
Positive obsession
Blunts pain,
Diverts rage,
And engages each of us
In the greatest,
The most intense
Of our chosen struggles.

OCTAVIA E. BUTLER, PARABLE OF THE TALENTS

Everyday Antiracism
Framework

Curiosity

Truth

Structure

Healing

Perception

Restitution

Belonging

Power

Contents

Prologue

I wrote the stories in this volume with the explicit aim of inspiring antiracist reflection and action. Having spent over thirty years seeking to influence social change through writing for scholarly and policy audiences, it was an absolute thrill to reactivate my long-dormant love of creative writing to produce these works of didactic fiction.

Confronting the racial inequity that permeates all facets of American life has motivated my professional career. My research and scholarship have focused on place-based approaches to urban equity and inclusion. The impact research center that I founded to advance and disseminate knowledge in this area, the National Initiative on Mixed-Income Communities at Case Western Reserve University, celebrated its tenth anniversary in 2023. After a year of reflection, reimagining, and recommitment, we renamed ourselves to better articulate our core mission. We are now NP3: Nurturing People. Power. Place.

Initially focusing on socioeconomic integration as an antipoverty strategy, I have increasingly incorporated a more explicit focus on race and racism. This led me to create a racial equity lens to guide thinking and action. My goal was to take a pragmatic, action-oriented approach to the daunting and despair-inducing topic of enduring anti-Black racism.

I identified four key constructs that could guide everyday action on racial equity: Curiosity, Structure, Perception, and Belonging. And then, in the season of racial reckoning that followed the police killings of George Floyd and Breonna Taylor, I added a racial justice lens with four more constructs: Truth, Healing, Restitution, and Power.

Together, these eight elements now make up my Everyday Antiracism framework. I am grateful to Mica Pollock who coined the phrase for the title of her 2008 edited handbook on race in schools. In this volume, each story takes up one of these elements and elucidates its meaning in fictional form.

Racial equity and racial justice are two related but very different concepts. I describe racial equity as Antiracism 1.0, the starting point for an antiracist journey. In contrast, racial justice can be considered something more like Antiracism 5.0, it is a far more profound threshold of social change. We can think of racial equity as "making it even," while we can think of racial justice as "making it right." Both are complex, monumental societal endeavors and both require a high degree of intentionality to make meaningful individual, collective, and systemic progress. Those of us seeking to practice everyday antiracism must have a clear sense of the difference and how to help advance each one.

To advance racial equity, and seek to "make it even," we must approach issues of race with a mindset of learning and discovery, we must identify systemic root causes of inequities, we must reveal and shift our implicit bias, and we must eliminate othering and promote inclusion. To work toward racial justice, and seek to "make it right," we must name and accept often ugly truths about our past, present, and future, we must help heal from racialized trauma, we must provide restitution to those who have been wronged, and we must shift control from the powerful to the vulnerable.

The characters in these stories demonstrate how this can be done and provide cautionary tales of the repercussions of failure to achieve this.

I push the notion of didacticism to the extreme in these stories, making the volume a blend of fiction and a how-to manual. Many of the stories contain specific examples of practices and even policies to advance antiracism. My fictional style intentionally has less nuance and more explicit exposition in order to err on the side of readers "getting it" and being inspired and guided to take specific action. Octavia Butler, science fiction maestro and queen of Afrofuturism, wrote just one volume of short stories, *Blood Child*. She included an afterword after each story, and I found that device tremendously informative to be able to learn about her inspirations and intentions for each story. I have borrowed that device here as an additional component of the didactic aims of the volume. I have also included questions after each story to guide reflection and discussion.

The volume title *Changing the Narrative* has several meanings. First, I am changing my narrative form from scholarly and policy writing to creative writing. Second, the overall theme of the volume is that to advance antiracism, we must change our prevailing narrative about the "other" and about the possibility of a more equitable and inclusive shared human existence. Third, within each story there is a moment of narrative or mindset shift for one or more of the characters. Finally, I have deployed a variety of narrative forms here, including first-person, second-person, and third-person narrators as well as a personal journal, an investigative journalism report, and the voice of God.

Enjoy *Changing the Narrative*.

The Passenger

F light 283 from Cleveland to Oakland was always packed. Unfortunately, on this particular Friday evening, even having all those passengers on board was not enough to prevent tragedy.

Carlos Rivera, Flight 283's pilot, projected warm energy as he welcomed passengers onto the plane. Even all these years into his flying career, he still buzzed with boyish zeal before every flight. As one of the rare Latino pilots that passengers would ever encounter, he made sure to stand just outside the cockpit during boarding to greet the oncomers. He enjoyed seeing the surprise in passengers' eyes as they encountered someone they did not expect to see in this role.

Smith Quentin was usually in the same state of body and mind as he strode down the gangway from the terminal onto the plane for this flight. Physically exhausted from another week of dawn until dusk activity at his gig. And mentally spent, but eagerly anticipating some time with his mom and high school buddies back in his hometown for the weekend. An astute observer would notice his patient demeanor despite the frequent pauses in the parade of onboarding passengers. The light caramel hue of his hoodie accentuated his dark chocolate complexion. His black jeans were stylish as were his sneakers which gleamed as if they had just been pulled out of their box. Two tastefully-sized diamond stud earrings sparkled as they reflected the overhead lights. With the lithe build of a hurdler and the smooth gait of a jazz musician, Smith stood out from the crowd and exuded a calm energy that had a soothing effect on those around him.

Smith's progress onto the plane paused once again as he passed by Pilot Rivera.

"Welcome aboard sir, thank you for flying with us this afternoon," Carlos stated as he nodded warmly.

"Hey man, good to be on board. Wow, not sure I've ever had a Latino pilot before. Can't be many of you guys, huh?" Smith queried with a friendly smile.

"We are just about five percent of all pilots, they tell me," Carlos responded with a wry grin. "But I've yet to see most of them. Enjoy the flight sir."

"Appreciate that my man, keep doin' you," Smith offered over his shoulder as the procession began to move on.

Carlos continued to gaze at Smith for a few additional moments. There was something familiar about the African American with his hair twisted neatly into short braids, his well-trimmed beard, and the rhythmic cadence of his confident stride. He shook his head, not being able to place the familiarity. Must be a famous musician or performer, he thought to himself.

Debbie McKinney, the experienced senior flight attendant, was standing right next to Carlos. She witnessed the exchange with Smith, and likewise lingered in her perusal of the graceful Black man as he moved down the aisle. Where have I seen him before, she wondered. Maybe she had encountered him on one of her countless previous flights, she surmised. But, then again, she had an insistent feeling that she had seen him speak. Or maybe she had read a magazine profile about him. Somehow, she felt that she knew something more about this guy. Well, maybe he's a famous athlete, she thought, he certainly moves like one.

Debbie turned her mind back to the tasks at hand. The flight was slightly delayed and she and her crew needed to keep the boarding process moving with the hope of making up some time once they got to their cruising altitude. Debbie operated with the knowing ease of a thirty-year veteran who had seen it all. Her sunny personality and her keen attention to detail made her a favorite team leader among flight attendants, who were usually thrilled to find out they had been assigned to her crew. Debbie had a natural ability to instill discipline while encouraging her crew members to enjoy their work together, even while conducting monotonous procedures, flight after flight.

She grabbed the intercom and made a cabin announcement:

"Ladies and gentlemen. Welcome aboard Flight 283 to Oakland. We're so glad to have you with us this evening and if you can get your bags into the overhead compartments quickly and take your seats, we're hoping to make up some of this delay and get you into the Bay Area close to the planned arrival time."

Debbie switched over to private mode to check in with her crew in the back of the Boeing 737.

"Alright people, let's get this baby loaded and get on our way. Frank and Joanna, put that delightful charm to work moving these folks along back there."

Frank Richman and Joanna Chung smiled knowingly to each other.

"How does she do that so smoothly?" Frank murmured, shaking his head. The creases around his eyes and deep dimples accentuated a face that was quick to smile.

"Tell us to move our asses, while giving us a compliment?" Joanna noted cheekily. She was the team member most likely to provide some lighthearted comic relief.

"Yup," said Frank, as he ushered a family of three into their row, and clicked shut an overhead bin that was already full. "Oh boy, master of the universe coming down the aisle in blue, I hope he's in your section," he whispered.

After years of flying together, Frank and Joanna had developed their own little game to entertain themselves, categorizing passengers as they boarded based on their appearance and mannerisms. Joanna looked up to check out the passenger Frank was referring to. A tall man in a crisply fitting navy blue suit who could have walked right off the cover of Fortune magazine strode imperiously down the aisle.

"Goddamn it, why do I always get the high and mighty corporate moguls?" Joanna hissed. "And here you go with a librarian, college professor, rabbi, and yoga teacher all lining up to be easy peasy customers of Café le Frank!"

Sure enough, a bookish, middle-aged woman with wire-rimmed glasses and graying hair pulled back into a tight bun, an older man in a tweed jacket with inquisitive eyes and a scraggly goatee, a pudgy, balding man with a peaceful, grandfatherly demeanor, and a limber woman in skintight leggings and brightly colored running shoes all filed dutifully into seats around Frank.

Smith was in another group of passengers just behind the foursome that Joanna had confidently categorized. Directly in front of him was an elderly White woman who was struggling to hoist her bag into the overhead bin. Smith reached to take her bag from her to help.

But as his brown hand came into view next to hers on her bag and she turned to see a tall Black man hovering over her, she instinctively flinched, gripped her bag more tightly, and pulled away, bumping into a teenager with a bulky backpack on the other side of her.

Smith softened his eyes, turned his palm over, and gestured gently to the woman. "Just offering to help you with your bag, ma'am."

"Oh! Well of course, that's so kind of you," the woman uttered, clearly trying to compose herself after the shock of the initial interaction. She settled into her aisle seat as Smith nestled her bag into the compartment and moved on down the plane. Peggy Irving loved to travel but was finding it harder and harder to fly by herself as she aged. She was headed to meet her first grandchild who had been born two months earlier to her daughter, a social work professor at UC Berkeley, and son-in-law, an animator at Pixar. Peggy had been beside herself with eagerness to meet her granddaughter, and she had been checking the days off on her wall calendar. She was a little embarrassed about her overreaction to Smith's kindly intrusion into her personal space and she berated herself quietly for her jumpiness.

Meanwhile at the front of the plane, Debbie and the fourth flight attendant Hazel Patrick had made good progress getting passengers into their places and were starting to check up and down the aisles to make sure that all baggage was properly stowed. Hazel had started her flight attendant career in her home country with Air Jamaica but had switched over to an American airline company when she had immigrated to the U.S. to join her husband in his hometown of Atlanta. As the most junior member of the crew, she was more thorough as she scanned each row, gently prompting passengers to push their bags further under their seats in her endearing island lilt.

"Ya know it caan go a little furtha than dat," she urged Smith with a smile and a wink as he settled into his window seat. He smiled back and complied, initially annoyed at being nagged, but soothed by Hazel's easygoing encouragement.

As she passed by Debbie, Hazel leaned in close and asked her "Can ya recognize de guy in 24F? Him look soooo familiah."

"I know what you mean," Debbie said softly, "I think he's a famous athlete, but I can't place him."

"Hmmm, me neithah," Hazel mused, "sure, ya must be right." She moved on with her tasks, still straining her mind to try to recall why the handsome Black passenger looked so familiar.

Smith's window seat was in the row with Joanna's presumed yoga instructor in the middle and college professor on the aisle. As soon as they were all seated, the yoga instructor, who was actually a gymnastics coach named Lizzie Stephens, turned to orient her body toward the professor and away from Smith, and began chatting away.

"What's that you're reading?" Lizzie asked the professor.

The professor, who was actually an insurance salesman named Sam Rollins, and just happened to be partial to tweed jackets, seemed pleasantly surprised at the attention from his cute seatmate. "It's a biography of FDR," he explained, "he's my favorite US president."

"Huh," said Lizzie, momentarily stymied by his choice of reading material, which held zero interest to her. Undeterred, she pivoted to another line of inquiry. "So where ya headed?"

"To an insurance convention in Sacramento," Sam said earnestly, "It's the highlight of my year and the chance to talk risk analysis and deductibles with fellow insurance guys."

"Huh." Lizzie said again, stymied for a beat longer this time. Taking a new tack, she launched into an unsolicited description of her trip to meet up with her former teammates from the University of San Francisco gymnastics team for a 10-year reunion.

Smith side-eyed this interchange between his seatmates with a mix of bemusement and light annoyance at being so obviously ignored. Imperceptibly he rolled his eyes and let out a long sigh borne of decades of experience being the invisible guy in most rooms. He smiled and thought to himself, makes it easier for me to get some sleep, as he put on his noise-cancelling headphones, slipped a plush neck pillow around his neck, and pulled a sleeping mask over his eyes.

As Frank did one more pass-through of the cabin, he did a double-take at Smith's row. Something poking out of Smith's bag under the seat in front of him had glinted in the light. As Frank looked more closely, he could see it was something metal and shiny.

Gesturing discreetly to Joanna, he nodded towards Smith's bag and raised his eyebrows, signaling that she should take a look herself. She did so and then they huddled to debrief in the back of the plane.

"Did you see that?" Frank asked.

"Well, it's clearly not cannabis or alcohol that we can confiscate from him and keep to ourselves, so I'm not very interested," Joanna smirked.

"Stop playing Joanna, I'm serious!" Frank insisted. "It could be a weapon of some kind."

"Oh gimme a break Frank," Joanna practically snorted, "a weapon that he somehow snuck through the security scanners?! C'mon man, get a grip. You can see he's some type of musician or performer – it's probably a musical instrument of some type, some kind of horn, I bet."

Frank chuckled sheepishly. "Yeah, he does look like a performer, doesn't he. OK, my bad, just being extra vigilant, like Debbie always tells us."

Joanna and Frank strapped themselves into their jump seats as the plane rumbled to a smooth takeoff.

Captain Rivera's voice came over the intercom: "Ladies and gentlemen, welcome aboard, once again. We're expecting a smooth, uneventful ride all the way into Oakland, so please sit back, relax and enjoy our four hour and thirty-minute flight."

The smooth, uneventful ride lasted only about half that long.

About two hours into the flight, Peggy, the new grandma, started to feel a tightening in her chest. Maybe it was just indigestion she told herself and straightened her seatback and adjusted her posture to try to ease the discomfort. But it only grew worse. She nudged the passenger next to her and asked him to ring the flight attendant's call button for her. One look at Peggy's growing distress and he complied quickly.

Hazel was the first one to reach Peggy.

"Yes ma'am, ya rang for sumthin?"

By now Peggy was clutching her chest and straining for breath. Hazel's eyes widened and she hustled back down the aisle to get Debbie. By the time she came back with Debbie, Frank and Joanna had also come over to check out the disturbance. At this point, Peggy could feel herself losing consciousness and she gripped the armrest tightly as her eyes fluttered shut. Debbie instructed Frank to tend to her as best he could and sent Joanna to the cockpit to alert the pilot.

Soon, Carlos' voice came over the intercom. "Ladies and gentlemen, we have a passenger on board who is in some medical distress. Do we have a doctor on board? If so, please ring your call button."

Up and down the aisle, passengers caught their breath and looked around anxiously. Everyone waited for five seconds, ten seconds, fifteen seconds, to see if a call button would ring.

No ring.

Carlos tried again. "If there is a doctor on board, please let us know by ringing your call button."

Another collective holding of breath. Another fifteen seconds with no ring.

"Ok each of you," Debbie directed Joanna and Hazel, "there are several sleeping passengers who may not have heard the announcement. Please check each row and ask if anyone is a doctor."

Joanna and Hazel each hustled off and started going row by row to ask if anyone was a doctor. Debbie asked Peggy's seatmates to move to the back of the plane so that she could lay the unconscious woman down across the seats. Frank started to perform CPR.

Joanna and Hazel returned having had no luck.

"You asked everyone?" Debbie asked, incredulous that on a flight of over 250 people, there was not a single physician to be found.

"Yes!" both exclaimed in unison.

Frank was now on his third round of CPR, but there was no reaction from Peggy's lifeless body.

Debbie tapped him gently on the back. "Frank honey," she said softly, "I'm afraid there's nothing else we can do."

Frank's shoulders slumped and Hazel started to sob and then shriek uncontrollably.

At that moment, Smith's eyes popped open as Hazel's wails penetrated his deep slumber. "Huh, wha-, what's happening?!" he asked Lizzie and Sam, who were looking somber next to him.

"That elderly lady a couple rows up just had a heart attack," Lizzie informed him sorrowfully.

"What?!?" Smith exclaimed.

He reached into his bag, got up from his seat, climbed past Lizzie and Sam, and stood in the aisle, stethoscope in hand.

"You're a, you're a, you're a doctor!?" Joanna stammered, her eyes wide with incredulity.

"He's a doctor!?" Hazel repeated, twisting her head from side to side to look at Debbie and at Frank.

Seeing Smith standing there in the aisle with the stethoscope in his hand, it suddenly dawned on each of the flight attendants and several of the other passengers where they had seen him before.

Dr. Smith Quentin was Newsweek's Person of the Year for his innovations to reduce heart surgery recovery time. He was the pride of The Cleveland Clinic cardiology department. He had made the rounds of daytime and late-night talk shows, lauded for his medical achievements and his life trajectory from a modest upbringing in public housing in Oakland.

Debbie grabbed Joanna by the arm and pulled her close. "I thought you asked everyone!?" she demanded.

"But, but, but, he didn't look like a doctor..." Joanna's voice trailed off as she realized the folly of her statement.

Smith leaned down to check Peggy's condition but soon stood back up and glared at the flight attendants and his fellow passengers. His head swiveled, eyes locking with each of them.

"What will it take for us to open our eyes?"

He paused, shaking his head, glanced at the stethoscope in his hand, and raised both hands out wide in a gesture that said, I've been right here in front of you all along.

"WHY DIDN'T ANYONE ASK ME?"

Flight 283 was eerily quiet the remainder of its abbreviated trip to land at the nearest airport.

One passenger would not see another day. Every other person on board would never be the same.

Author's Reflection

I hope you enjoyed the first story in this volume. Although the stories were not written in the order in which they appear, The Passenger was the first story I wrote. So, it holds a special place in my heart as the first short story, and the first antiracist fiction, I ever wrote.

The idea for a themed volume of short stories came to me on a plane flight. And as I sat mulling over what I could write a story about, the plot and denouement and title of The Passenger came to me very quickly.

Like each of the stories you can read here, this story revealed itself to me quite effortlessly. I've come to understand, through writing this volume, that these stories exist already, in some liminal psychological space of experience and meaning, waiting for me to be ready to serve as a vessel to bring them into narrative existence. I realize now that many, perhaps all, creatives (and I've never before thought of myself as a creative!) feel this way about the artistic process. We get to bring into our reality something that has been waiting in another existential plane (for sure, no pun intended!).

I have experienced the dynamics of The Passenger for decades now. As a Black man who flies often, I have evolved from annoyance, to hurt, to bemusement, as I experience a heightened sense of being invisible and being avoided in the tight and routinized confines of a plane flight.

I am a Southwest Rapid Rewards member and thus, as those of you who have flown Southwest know, have regularly experienced a unique sociological experiment that happens every time I take a Southwest flight. On Southwest, there are no pre-assigned seats, every single passenger gets to select where they sit, or, more to the racialized point, who they sit next to. There are undoubtably many factors that go into split second seat selection as passengers hustle onto a Southwest plane. I, for example, do not sit in the front third of the plane due to a slight claustrophobia I've developed in my older years. But invariably, dear reader, believe you me, the seats next to me sit unfilled long after the other rows have filled up. Black folks immediately resonate with this fact, some of my White friends and colleagues have had to see it for themselves to believe it.

Not only am I avoided, but there is a lack of curiosity about me. Truth be told, all of us headphone-wearing, screen-scrolling addicts display a lack of curiosity about those around us. But I've often wondered what a revelation it would be for people's assumptions about me to be disrupted. Contrast the airplane context with Uber rides, where my drivers invariably express their surprise to discover that I am a professor. I've heard some version of "I've never met a Black professor before!" numerous times.

So, this story is inspired by my experiences and invites readers to consider what if our lack of curiosity had fatal consequences.

How might you deepen your curiosity, particularly about those different from you?

What is the role of curiosity, or lack thereof, in race relations?

When might you ask a question as the starting point for a conversation about race, rather than making a statement?

The Dark
Chocolate Boys of
the Class of 2005

H ow had these twenty years passed so quickly?

Bradford Myers crossed his hands behind his head and leaned back in his leather office chair. Placing his well-polished wingtips up on his mahogany desk, he gazed out of his massive 42nd floor office window at the gleaming Chicago skyline and sparkling blue lake beyond. Another gorgeous spring day in one of the world's greatest cities. And what a perch from which to be savoring his good fortune.

Man, he was looking forward to his high school reunion this weekend! How far he and his four best friends had come since graduating from Ebony Scholars Prep Academy, Chicago's innovative high school for Black boys. Their career journeys had proceeded steadily upward, each entering professions that aligned well with their passions and their personalities. And now they were each at the top of their games. The only downside of how far each of them had risen into leadership roles was that they were now spread across the country and rarely got to see each other in person.

He felt a slight chill and shivered, which was strange given that he was in a full suit and tie and had just adjusted his office thermostat up a couple notches. He stood and ticked it up a couple more degrees. He also noted that his back was sore and twisted in both directions, then leaned forwards and backwards to stretch it out a bit. He sat back in his chair then returned to his reclining position.

He reminisced about the days when he and the guys were inseparable. They took as many of the same classes as possible and gathered for some raucous fun at the same lunch table each day. They all played on the school's state championship soccer team, and each afternoon after practice they would be at one or another of their homes, studying and playing video games.

He chuckled thinking about how it all began. The fall of their first year of high school, five dark brown dudes, all nervously sitting around a detention room table, looking at each other.

Brad had spoken first, he always had the instinct to lead. "Well, well, well. What are the chances of the five darkest brothers in this joint all getting on the wrong side of the law at the same time?" They had all chuckled and shaken their heads knowingly.

"Who you calling dark, sitting over there looking like a fudge brownie!" one of the other boys had replied.

"You got it," Brad had replied smoothly, "I like to think of myself. . ." he paused for effect, " . . .as dark chocolate." The boys had squealed with laughter. He had continued, "And the girls sure love themselves some dark chocolate!"

The name, and the camaraderie, had stuck. They began calling themselves the Dark Chocolate Boys. DC Boys for short. And each boy got a nickname that started with DC. Bradford was DC Biz, because it was clear that he would have a career in business. Always calculating how to leverage one thing into two more things. Always the first one to see an entrepreneurial opportunity and the only one willing to take the risk to seize it. Why have a boring old lemonade stand, when you could make lemon slushies and charge twice as much? Why just make and sell t-shirts for homecoming weekend when you could make and sell t-shirts, hats, jackets, scarfs *and* socks? He was tailor-made for the corporate world. It was no surprise to any of them that, after an undergraduate degree from Morehouse College and an MBA from Harvard, he was now President and CEO of a highly successful investment banking firm, Aya Capital Investors.

His cell phone buzzed. He smiled as he checked the caller's name. Yup, no surprise that Mike would be the first to respond to the group text he had sent out this morning.

My Dark Chocolate Brothas! The weekend is upon us. Twenty years?!? Gimme a holla when you can so we can pin down some final details.

Michael Modlin. Known among their crew as DC Med since he had always wanted to be a doctor. Mike was the most organized and disciplined of their group. Always making to do lists and ticking off his daily tasks. The guys were constantly ribbing him, then and now, for not being able to just relax and go with the flow. "But what's the plan guys?" was his constant refrain. Trained as an orthopedic surgeon at the University of Chicago, he had risen to be one of the top knee reconstruction specialists in the country. His passion and precision had drawn him into the quality control arena. He was now the Chief Quality Officer at Johns Hopkins Hospital in Baltimore, where he combined his executive duties with continued surgery practice.

"DC Med! My guy!" Brad bellowed as he answered his phone.

"What's up DC Biz. You good my man?" Mike responded flatly. Brad could hear the bone-tiredness in Mike's voice. He wondered how many surgeries and how many executive meetings he had led that week.

"I'm real good Mike. Can't wait to get you into town and make sure you relax and recharge bit," Brad said with that big brother tone he always took on with the guys. "Listen, I'll make this quick. I know you're crazy busy. I just need to confirm that you can make it in on time to catch the Bulls game Friday night and whether I should get a ticket for you to the Earth, Wind and Fire concert on Sunday?"

"Wouldn't miss either one DC Biz! Count me in." Mike now sounded like he was smiling broadly.

"Ok man – safe travels in."

"Love you bro. Appreciate ya always keeping us on point."

"That's what I do! Later!" Brad hung up, smiling and shaking his head. How many of their fellas' get-togethers would not have happened without him wrangling the guys together? But he deeply respected the passion each of the guys had for their careers and felt blessed to be able to help keep them connected.

Their twenty-year reunion. Wow. The theme that Ebony Scholars Academy had selected for this milestone occasion, Celebrating the Path: All That Brought You to This Moment, had really gotten him thinking.

In the case of him and his friends, the path had started even before they were born. Each of their mothers had received pre-natal care with biweekly visits from a home health worker. His mom often talked about the trust she had developed in that caring professional who had come to feel like an older sister. All the things she never would have thought of that were good for the baby on the way and all the things to be avoided.

He recalled his mother telling him how she had developed a special sense of community with other expectant moms at the free parenting classes at the local library. With his dad never a presence in their lives, she described the peer support and accountability as invaluable. She had formed lifelong friendships with some of the women from those parenting classes and they had continued to share resources at each stage of their children's lives. It was one of those moms who had encouraged his mother to apply for an early childhood subsidy so that he could attend the high-quality early learning center in their neighborhood which would have been otherwise unaffordable. And she often talked about how much she had gained from the work she had done at the center as a part of the volunteer commitment which all parents, regardless of subsidy, were expected to make. How wild to find that all five of their moms had benefited from the same combination of prenatal, peer-to-peer, and early childhood learning resources.

Celebrating the path.

He shouldn't forget the housing support that had been provided to his mom when she lost her job. A subsidized unit in a beautiful new inclusionary housing complex had given them a solid home base from which to stabilize their lives and exposed them to an array of neighbors from a wide range of backgrounds.

He thought about Ms. Maria, their Puerto Rican next door neighbor who had initially kept her distance and then came to be like a godmother to him. "Bradford," she told him once, "all my life I've been told the worst things about your people and I was so scared when you moved in here about what that would mean for our peaceful complex. Instead we've learned so much from each other, your mom and I. There was so much I didn't understand about the unfairness of our society. And I thought I knew how to cook before your mom started schooling me!"

His phone buzzed again. Lemme guess, he thought to himself before looking at the caller's name, next up should be Roger. Sure enough, it was Roger Knight. DC Tech. The guy who always had to have the latest gadgets and technology. Always taking things apart to see how they worked and then nimbly putting them back together as if he had been there when they were assembled. Always envisioning the over-the-horizon technology that would one day become commonplace. What if your cell phone could be your camera? Check. What if you could talk to your stereo? Check. What if cars could drive themselves? Check. One of his earliest memories of Roger was when his mom refused to buy him an air conditioner and so he jerry-rigged one for himself out of a plastic tub filled with ice, some piping, and the fan that his mom had given him. He had even connected the fan's remote control to a thermometer to create an auto-activation when the temperature rose above a certain level.

Now Roger was the CEO of AI for Equity, a tech company he launched to focus on the use of artificial intelligence to even the playing field for entrepreneurs of color. His company's products helped small businesses vastly increase the sophistication of their finance, marketing, communications, and other core functions at a fraction of the conventional cost.

"DC Tech! Talk to me bruh. What city in the world are you calling me from?" Brad was well-used to Roger constantly globetrotting in a quest for investors and clients.

"I'm in Copenhagen, my man. But I'll be headed for Chi-town the day after tomorrow, don't worry." Brad could envision Roger multitasking as they were talking. "I got your email DC Biz, I'm good for the Bulls game and you know I would *not* miss Earth, Wind and Fire."

"My guy! Glad to hear it DC Tech. Can't wait to see you man." Brad was relieved that Roger was able to prioritize attending this fellas weekend.

"Ok, gotta roll, see you on Friday!" Roger was off the line before Brad could respond.

Twenty years. All that brought you to this moment. It had indeed been a wondrous journey with supportive resources at every turn.

He thought back to their school days together. Roger was constantly on the move. Come to think of it, all five of them had juggled schedules full of stimulating extracurriculars, thanks to Ebony Scholars Academy. It all started with the carefully-selected and well-trained guidance counselors who were like advisors, coaches, therapists, confidantes and concierges all rolled into one. Whereas he often heard from his Black peers at other schools about guidance counselors telling them what they could *not* do - Are you sure you want to try that advanced placement course? Do you really want to waste an application to an Ivy League school? – the guidance counselors at Ebony Scholars Academy were constantly setting stretch goals for the young men.

And the classes were where the true magic happened. Teachers were extensively trained in differentiated learning techniques so that there was no tracking at Ebony Scholars Academy, no gifted classes, no remedial classes. Having two instructors was vital, each teacher and teacher's aide were skilled at delivering the material concurrently at a variety of levels of difficulty and depth so that each student could engage at the level they were most ready for. And those students who were most advanced were encouraged to help other students learn, supporting others while sharpening their own ability to articulate the concepts.

And there was no special treatment or lower academic expectations for student-athletes. In fact, Ebony called their athletic staff "scholar-coaches" and made sure they remained fully briefed on the current focus of the school curriculum in order to incorporate elements of it into their daily sports practices. On an Ebony sports team, students could expect coaches to emphasize the mathematical concepts in their play-calling and use literature and poetry to inspire teamwork.

And Ebony Scholars Academy tended to the mental health of its students as much as their academic and physical development. Regular sessions with a therapist were normalized from the moment the boys arrived at the school. Many of the boys came from traumatic childhood contexts characterized by violence, loss, and grief, so the school emphasized a healing-centered approach that built plenty of time into each day for self-regulation. Yoga and mindfulness were features of many class sessions and the colors, music, and plants throughout the school were carefully selected to promote calm and a sense of restoration.

He had long recognized that the feature that topped it all off was the bridge into college. Ebony staff had drilled into the students from day one that college was the next destination for every single one of them. There were colorful pennants from hundreds of colleges displayed in every room of the school, even the bathrooms. Visits to college campuses started freshman year, not junior year like Brad's friends from other schools. And it seemed that students from local colleges were constantly in his classrooms and afterschool activities. By the time he was a senior not only did he have a clear idea of his top college choices, but he had a deep understanding of the college experience and its challenges and opportunities.

He was fully ready for Morehouse College when he arrived in Atlanta, and also ready to take full advantage of the college support phone line that Ebony Scholars Academy made available to all of its students. He had used the line almost weekly during his freshman year in college. His mom, who had not graduated high school, would not have known the answers to most of the questions he posed to the Ebony alums who volunteered their time to staff the support line. Even his senior year, he was still calling into the line from time to time for guidance and insight. Several of his early investors at Aya Capital were Ebony alums he had met through the support line.

What a comprehensive educational experience he had received, Brad marveled. He was really looking forward to being back on the Ebony Scholars Academy campus. Such great memories.

He suddenly shivered and felt a strange wave of coldness flow over him. What was up with the overactive air conditioning? And he could swear it felt more moist and even dank in his office. He sniffed the air. Could the air ducts be developing a mold problem? He'd have to remember to have maintenance look into it. He also felt the strain in his back worsening, had he pulled a muscle working out yesterday?

Another buzz of his phone brought a smile back to his face. Let's see, he mused, who would be next, and then who would be the last to check in?

Ha! The person who would be the *last* to call was easy to predict. That would be the most absent-minded and self-absorbed of the bunch – DC Deep, the academic, Prof. Malcolm Briggs.

That meant this next call had to be the social activist of the crew, and minister at one of the most influential Black churches in the country – the Reverend Dr. Otis Dwight James, Senior Pastor of Farlough Presbyterian Church in Atlanta, GA.

He checked the caller's name. Sure enough, it was Otis.

"DC Preach!" Brad shouted, "I appreciate you pausing from saving the world and saving souls to give your guy a holla."

"DC Biz, it's been way too long," Otis replied in his soothing baritone, which always helped Brad feel more at peace. "My apologies for not getting back to you earlier. Man, this exploratory campaign stuff is no joke." Otis was considering a run for U.S. Senate, and in addition to his regular church and civic duties, had been crisscrossing the state building his name recognition and galvanizing support from donors.

"No worries Rev," Brad assured him, "just as long as you're calling me with what I want to hear."

"Oh, I got you Brad," Otis boomed, "I would not miss this reunion for the world. And these Bulls tickets and the Earth, Wind and Fire concert? Man, you sure know how to sweeten the deal! I'm all in brother. See you Friday."

"Can't wait DC Preach – see you then!"

He chuckled again to himself, imagining Otis, Roger, and Mike and how secure they each seemed in their careers. Well, it sure had not happened by accident. Ebony Scholars Academy had prided itself on early and consistent career exposure for its students. A large group of Black male professionals had been recruited to serve as career mentors to the students. Guidance counselors helped match mentors to students according to their interests and students met with their mentors every two weeks. Students were assigned a new mentor each year and encouraged to stay in touch with the previous ones. By the time he was a senior in high school, Brad had been mentored by an accountant, a lawyer, and a Fortune 500 CEO.

The City of Chicago had adopted a Baby Bonds Initiative the year before he and the guys were born, so they were one of the first cohorts to receive a matched college saving account at birth, with a starting balance of $1,000, into which the city would match every dollar saved by the student's family. And hands-on financial literacy had been built into every stage of education that he could remember: money counting and banking games in pre-school, tracking the stock market in elementary school, simulations about managing household finances and running a business in high school.

Celebrating the path.

He had not appreciated at the time how much careful thought had gone into lining up all these supports that he and his mom had taken advantage of. It had just felt like the system was in place to help guide him to success. It felt so natural and routine, but in retrospect he could see that it was anything but. An entire partnership network had conspired to weave together a cradle-to-career pipeline for him and his peers. Government services, non-profit programs, faith-based efforts, private volunteers and donors. Amazing.

Another shiver. And this time he could swear he felt a drop of water splash on his head. He rubbed his head and his hand came away wet. Aha! But when he scanned the ceiling, he could see no sign of dripping water. How very strange. And why was his back aching so much? He'd have to take it easy on the partying this weekend. Good luck achieving that with the fellas around.

As if on cue, his phone buzzed.

He didn't even check the caller's name before he answered. "DC Deep, I presume?"

"Man, Brad, sorry, the day got away from me my guy," Malcolm explained in his usual speedy cadence, "I started running a new experiment and the next thing you know..."

Brad interrupted, "Deep, my man, your days *always* get away from you. That's how you roll. If you didn't have to eat, or sleep, or talk to other human beings..."

"DC Biz, you know me way too well, that does sound kinda nice," Malcolm agreed. "So remind me, is the reunion *this* weekend?"

"Malcolm, please tell me you are messing with me," Brad implored.

"Let's just say I am, how about that, since I'm sensing that it is indeed this weekend. Whooo time flies! Ok, yeah count me in for the game and the concert and lemme hop off and get my plane flight booked."

Brad shook his head, "DC Deep, some things just do not change." They hung up.

Dr. Malcolm Briggs was an experimental psychologist at Stanford and the world's foremost expert on empathy. He ran an Empathy Lab and was rumored to be well on his way to a Nobel Prize for his breakthrough discoveries on the biological and social determinants of human capacity for empathy. The most bookish of the group by far, it had always been clear that Malcolm was destined for a life of research and scholarship. Brad had never seen anyone devour books the way Malcolm did. In their afterschool hangout sessions, Malcolm always finished his homework first, never wanted to join them for video games, and always dug into a book as soon as he could. But he always sat near them, never seemed distracted by the antics and noise, and Brad often caught Malcolm taking a pause in his reading and grinning at whatever goofiness the guys were up to.

He sighed deeply. Okay, cool, he'd heard from all the guys and the plans for the weekend were set. Suddenly, the flurry of calls and boost of anticipatory energy had him feeling very tired. He leaned back in his office chair, propped his feet on the desk, closed his eyes, and dozed off.

A drop of water splashed on his forehead. And then another one.

The third one woke him up.

He opened his eyes and was filled with a deep sense of dread.

He was in a small, dark room lying on a hard metal bed. His whole body ached. There was condensation on the walls and on the ceiling. The room smelled dank and moldy. A thin blanket had fallen onto the floor leaving him shivering.

The fuzziness of sleep slowly cleared from his mind. The vivid career successes of the Dark Chocolate Boys faded. And the devastating truth left him gasping for breath, bitter tears of despair rolling down his cheeks.

Prison.

Yes, he was part of a brotherhood who called themselves the Dark Chocolate Boys.

But the dark complexions that bound each of them in solidarity had signaled danger and untrustworthiness to society, and placed barrier after barrier in their lives.

They each had difficult and traumatizing life paths into the failing high school where they met. Only two of them had made it through graduation, and none had attended college.

Bradford was indeed the leader of the Dark Chocolate Boys. But his leadership had led them all to their current fate.

Their winding path after high school in and out of demeaning, low-wage jobs led to the highly misguided decision to participate in a check-cashing scheme using counterfeit U.S. Treasury Checks. He had encouraged all of them to participate. It was not long before the scheme was uncovered as a part of a far-reaching FBI investigation. A federal offense for fraud and identity theft resulted in thirty years in prison for him and each of his co-conspirators.

As his glorious dream faded and the shock of being wrenched back to his tragic reality wore off, Bradford chuckled derisively to himself about the folly of the utopian lifepath his mind had somehow concocted. C'mon man, that truly was some wild dream! That could never, ever, ever, happen. Not in this racist ass country.

He pulled the threadbare blanket back over himself, closed his eyes, and tried to savor the lingering remnants of the evaporating dream.

It had all made so much sense. It had felt so solid. And so reasonable.

He thought about all the contributions to society the Dark Chocolate Boys could have been able to make, paying back the social investments in them many times over.

Why *wasn't* it possible?

Why?

Author's Reflection

As an author, I relished the process of crafting the steady build to the gut punch twist at the end of this story. As a Black man in America, I felt immensely sad and desolate to have to end the story in that way.

So much Black and Brown talent wasted on the sidelines and in the prisons of American society. Oh, what could be!

This story, along with *Doing it Our Way* and *It's a Power Thing*, is one where my didactic fiction style is most evident. I use some of these stories to spell out in detail my ideas for exactly how we could do better as a society. Action-oriented!

It was a joy to have the opportunity to fabricate a plot device through which I could lay out my own comprehensive prescription for how to counteract structural racism in America.

While this is fictionalized, it draws on and depicts many practices that are currently happening in cities across America. Hopefully it felt concrete and actionable to you.

Why couldn't we do this?

What practices did you find most compelling here?

What steps could you personally take in your spheres of influence to work towards implementing one or more of these practices?

Awakening

P^{lease help me do this with grace and compassion.}

Please help me do this with grace and compassion.

Michelle prayed silently to herself as the taxi pulled to a stop. She surveyed the condition of her childhood home, seeing it for the first time since she left for college two years earlier.

She gave the airline ticket envelope in her hand one more glance and tapped it gently with a smile. Then she tucked it into her bag before getting out of the taxi.

She looked up and down the street while the taxi driver retrieved her bags from the trunk. She was a tall, large-framed woman who would stand out in any crowd for the confident ease with which she moved, her observant hazel brown eyes, and a bold hairstyle with two big afro puffs on either side of her head. She wore khaki shorts and a black Nina Simone t-shirt with the singer activist staring assertively ahead, as if daring anyone to mess with her. Michelle's self-assured stance as she scanned the block made clear that this was her home turf.

Not much had changed on Cumberland Street. She felt a warm sense of familiarity that was quickly followed by a pang of exasperation. The sidewalk was cracked and crumbling on both sides of the street. The street itself was badly in need of paving. The taxi driver had groaned as he weaved the car through the potholes. There were almost as many vacant lots on the street as there were homes. These overgrown lots were strewn with litter, some with larger items like tires and broken furniture. She could see some kind of appliance, maybe a fridge, lying on its side on the lot across the street.

She chuckled to see that the large *Jesus Saves! Jesus Loves You....* mural was still there, painted on the side wall of an abandoned store building on the corner. She had always appreciated that the artist had ended the proclamation with the four dots, which felt like an invitation for the reader to take action to claim the proffered love. *Jesus Loves You....* your turn! When she was a child skipping down the street to catch the school bus, she used to find the mural comforting. It fit as one more evangelical puzzle piece with saying grace before dinner, coloring in her Noah's Ark storybook during her mom's Wednesday evening bible study group, and falling asleep hearing her grandmother humming old spirituals.

Shaking her head and sighing deeply, she considered how much her sensibilities had evolved in just a couple of years. She now saw the deep irony in the mural's proclamation of Jesus' compassion amid such enduring urban decay. Now the four dots seemed to open a much more complex issue. Faith has the power to sustain community members' hope and solidarity while also pacifying them to accept their current conditions. A period at the end of the statement would have expressed certainty. *Jesus Loves You.* The four dots now seemed to ask, *Jesus Loves You...*so why you got to live like this?

Of the eight neighboring houses she could see from where she was standing, three appeared to be abandoned. The closest one was in the roughest condition. The porch roof was propped up with a wood beam wedged diagonally from the roof into the ground. Two of the second floor windows had broken glass and a third window looked wide open. The side yard, surrounded by a tall rusting metal fence, was filled with furniture, appliances, and numerous sheets of wood.

Strikingly, the house immediately next to this abandoned house looked like it could have been in any affluent suburb in America. Freshly painted with a warm shade of peach and bright white window trim, the house looked like a doll's house that had been magically supersized. The front lawn was lush green and carefully manicured, the kind that compels you to kick off your shoes and walk barefoot across it. There was no one sitting in the carefully arranged furniture on the front porch, but it was not hard to imagine neighbors sharing laughter and stories as they kept an eye on children playing in the front yard.

Which house best told the story of the trajectory of this block? Michelle mused. And what did this juxtaposition of care and neglect say about the society that allowed such disparity and about the neighborhood residents who accepted it as normal?

"You gonna keep your momma waiting for her hug?" The sound of her mother's voice pulled Michelle out of her rumination, touching a tender place deep inside her.

"Hey mom!" Michelle turned with a broad smile and hustled over to be enveloped in a joyful hug by her mother. Maya Johnson was as tall as her daughter, but thinner, and her hair was pulled back in a tight bun that gave an aura of discipline and focus. The caring and attentive competence she projected might have led an observer to guess that she was a librarian, or a school nurse.

In fact, she was the office manager at a dentist's office, a position she had held for well over twenty years. When the dentist's office had changed ownership a few years back, the new leadership had quickly recognized her skills and dependability and convinced her to stay on in her position. Early in her life, she had aspired to be a medical professional herself. But when her marriage to Michelle's father ended in divorce after only four years, she'd been drawn to the stability of life as an office administrator. And she had dedicated herself to showering her only child with love and affection.

"My baby's home, my baby's home," Maya chanted as she squeezed Michelle tightly and rocked back and forth. Michelle squeezed back just as tightly and allowed herself to feel a sense of vulnerability and dependence that she had kept at bay since she left home.

Maya pulled away slightly, looked Michelle up and down, and then pulled her back in for another tight hug. Michelle smiled and fully relished the moment. She had yearned for the warmth of her mother's embrace, perhaps even more than she had realized. And she knew that the visit would not sustain this carefree mood. So, she leaned in willingly.

"Ok Shelley, let's get my baby in this house where she belongs!" Maya said as she grabbed one of Michelle's bags and strode up the stairs to the front door.

Shelley. Michelle had not told anyone at college about her child-hood nickname. College had provided an opportunity for a sharp break from her past which she had seized wholeheartedly. Hearing the nickname generated mixed feelings. The comfort of her mother's love. And a pull backwards to an identity and a state of youthful ignorance she had left behind for good.

Where she belongs, her mother had said. Unsure if this was just her mother's exuberance or a poke at her decision to go so far away to college, Michelle decided to give her mother the benefit of the doubt on this one. She held onto the warm, comfortable feeling of the welcome hug just a little longer.

Inside, the house looked and felt just like she remembered. In fact, as she stood in the foyer and scanned the first floor, she could not see a single thing that had changed. She suddenly had an eerie feeling that time had stood still inside this house the entire period that she had been away. She shook off the feeling, once again consciously deciding to avoid saying anything critical that would put her mother on the defensive, yet.

They took her luggage up the stairs and into her bedroom, which also looked precisely as she left it two years earlier.

"I did not move a thing!" Maya proclaimed proudly with a broad smile and outstretched arms, "Nothing has been changed here, my sweet girl." *But your sweet girl has changed so much*, Maya thought to herself, biting her lip.

"I'll leave you to settle in and freshen up," Maya instructed, "C'mon down as soon as you're set, I've got my special lasagna hot and ready for you. Bennett College may have lured my daughter away from me, but I know they ain't got a lasagna as yummy as your momma's!"

"Oh momma, you sure know how to make a woman feel welcome," Michelle replied, noting that her mother's eyebrows raised slightly at her calling herself a "woman." Michelle waited to see if a response was coming, but her mom turned with a barely perceptible shake of her head and went down the stairs.

With her bedroom to herself, it was Michelle's turn to shake her head as she took stock of the decorations and belongings and realized how familiar yet how offputting most of them seemed to her. And some things were downright offensive to her now. First off, the pink and powder blue color scheme of the room felt almost nauseating.

How had she made it through all those years with these colors? Would it be worth the fight to see if her mom would let her paint her room red, black and green, the colors of the African American flag?

She was very surprised to see that the posters on her walls had far more White people than people of color. Lady Gaga, Katy Perry, NSYNC and the Backstreet Boys. It was hard to imagine a time when these were her preferred performers. Even the Black performers she had chosen to spotlight were mainly light-skinned. Beyonce, Rihanna, Janet Jackson, and Michael Jackson at his lightest and whitest. Though she was still a fan of Martin Lawrence, the poster with his broad grin and exaggeratedly wide eyes now struck her as reminiscent of the Stepin Fetchit minstrel character from the 1940s.

And then there was her Barbie collection. She could not help but smile at the memory of countless hours spent playing make-believe with her Barbies. But why had she been so content with so many White Barbies and just a single Black Barbie? And why wasn't the Black one her favorite one? And why hadn't she questioned why her only guy Barbie was her White Ken doll?

And how had she not rebelled against her mom's decision to put up an image of White Jesus above the headboard of her bed?

Once again, her mom's voice brought her back to the present moment. "Shelley, honey, c'mon on down for dinner! Please come while it's hot."

Michelle took a deep breath and released a long exhale. *Lord, be with me as I have this conversation with my mother*, she whispered. She glanced at the image above her headboard, *White Jesus, I'll even take your help too!* She couldn't help grinning at her little joke.

"And what are you grinning about, young lady?" Maya queried as Michelle took her seat at the dining table.

"Oh, I'm just glad to be home momma," Michelle replied.

She bowed her head as her mom began to say grace. "Lord, thank you for bringing my baby girl back to her momma where she belongs. Thank you for the full scholarship that you made possible. Thank you for all the learning she is doing at college and for all the people who are looking out for her. And thank you for keeping her safe until she can return home to start her career. Bless this food and may it nourish our bodies. Amen."

"Amen," Michelle responded as she dug into her lasagna eagerly.

"So, Shelley." Maya's voice took on a stern quality.

"Yes, momma?" Michelle looked up from her plate.

"I just gotta ask you." Maya paused as if feeling a little conflicted about what she was about to say.

"Uh huh, momma?" Michelle could guess where this was headed.

"Baby, why did it take you two years to come home to visit me?" As the pain of abandonment spread across Maya's face, she looked more aged and worn. "Each time I've asked you during our phone calls, I felt like you were not being fully real with me."

Michelle kept chewing slowly. And there it was. The question she knew would be coming. She was not at all surprised that her mother had wasted no time getting straight to her main concern.

Well, she was ready and had been rehearsing her answer for weeks.

"I missed you momma, I really did. I missed your laughter, I missed our walks, and I missed watching goofy movies with you." Michelle paused for effect. "And Lord have I missed your cooking!"

She scooped another chunk of lasagna into her mouth.

"And being away from you helped me see all the amazing things about you," she continued.

"Ok Shelley, don't be trying to butter me up, you know I'm not falling for that!" Maya said with a wry grin.

"No really momma," Michelle interrupted. "I never fully appreciated how kind you are, how truly giving you are. I thought all mothers put others before themselves and made their children feel like the most special people in the world. But so many of my friends at school felt like they were not their mom's utmost priority."

She turned her attention to the salad nestled around the lasagna on her plate and popped a cherry tomato into her mouth.

"And I always felt like I could open up to you and you would hear me out." Michelle smiled warmly. "My friends helped me see that you and I have something very rare, most of them would never tell their mothers half the stuff I have told you."

Maya was also smiling broadly. "That is lovely to hear Shelley. I'm so glad you feel like I did right by you."

Michelle hated to disrupt the positive feeling, but now was the moment of truth.

"Well actually momma, that's the thing."

"Baby?"

"You've done your absolute best and you've had the most caring intentions."

"But...?" Maya asked, apprehensively.

Michelle sat up in her chair and leaned forward. "But there are ways in which I now see that you have not done right by me. Or done right by yourself."

Michelle winced as she watched the delight vanish from her mother's face, replaced by a look of dismay.

"Shelley! Baby! How can you possibly say that!?"

"Momma, you....we, we have perceptions and mindsets inside of us, that cause us to think we are inferior to White people and undeserving of all that life has to offer." Michelle tried to soften her eyes as she expressed this harsh truth.

"Inferior to White people?" Maya sputtered as she pushed her plate away from her.

"Undeserving?" She clenched her teeth and narrowed her eyes. "Young lady, you had better explain yourself! You know your mother is a proud Black woman, how can you say this?!"

Time to go all the way, Michelle thought to herself. She finished the bite of lasagna she was chewing and wiped her mouth with her napkin.

"Momma, what do you call the front room of our house?" Michelle pointed towards the front of the house. "The room with the furniture that you keep the plastic covering over."

"Michelle," Maya rolled her eyes, "what does that have to do with anything?"

Michelle stared intently at her mother. "Momma, please just answer the question. What have you called that room the whole time I was growing up?"

Maya sighed and closed her eyes, a realization dawning on her.

"'The White Room,'" she whispered softly.

"I didn't hear you momma, what did you say?" Michelle asked dramatically.

"I said I called it 'The White Room.'" Maya stated firmly, with a frown.

"And why momma?" Michelle pressed.

"Because it is the one room in the house that I keep in pristine condition, the best room in the house, the room we go in only when guests are here," Maya said sadly. "My momma and grandma had a White Room in their house as well."

"And why did you all call it 'White' momma?" Michelle pressed again.

"Oh Shelley," Maya said deflatedly.

"Momma, why call it 'White'?"

"Because...because White people have the best stuff. If it's White, it's better."

"And if it's Black, it's worse," Michelle added.

"No Michelle! I never said that!" Maya declared.

"Oh no?" Michelle exclaimed, her voice rising. "What about my 7th grade boyfriend, Alfred Jenkins? Do you remember what you said about him?"

"Yeah," Maya admitted readily, "I said he was a nice boy, but he was so dark-skinned, I wondered why you chose him."

"Yes you did," Michelle agreed. "Poor Alfred figured out why you never warmed up to him. And momma, why did you encourage me to play volleyball instead of basketball?"

"Because the basketball team had only Black girls on it," Maya confessed, "I was worried it would be too Black of an experience for you, and would hold you back."

"And what did you ask me about Bennett College when I got the scholarship and told you it was my top choice?" Michelle inquired.

"Oh Shelley, I don't remember," Maya sighed, sounding extremely tired.

"Well, I sure do. You asked how it could possibly be as good an education when it served only Black women, compared to the White schools I had been admitted to. And what did you say when I told you that I had selected Africana Studies as my major?"

"Shelley, I had never heard of Africana Studies!" Maya protested.

"Of course you hadn't momma. But what did you say?" Michelle asked.

Maya's face was downcast. "I asked how you were going to get a job after studying that Black stuff."

"Yes you did momma."

Maya looked at Michelle insistently. "But Shelley, I've always just wanted the best for you."

Michelle took a long steady look into her mother's eyes. Her face conveyed a deep seriousness of purpose. "Actually momma, I've come to realize that your own deep-down acceptance of the myth that Black people are inferior, has led you to hold me back from pursuing my truly best self."

"Shelley, how dare you!" Maya exclaimed as she jumped up from the table, stood glaring at Michelle for a moment, then stormed out of the dining room.

Michelle's shoulders slumped. This was just as hard as she had anticipated. But it also felt really good to be confronting the negative inner perceptions her mom had been holding onto for so long.

She cleared the table, put the leftover food away, and washed the dishes. Her long day of travel and the emotional weight of the conversation was catching up to her and she felt very tired. The house was quiet and dark, and she figured her mom had headed to bed for the evening, so she did the same.

***

Michelle came downstairs the next morning to the delicious smells of breakfast wafting through the house. A pot of her favorite oatmeal with bananas and strawberries sat on the stove. Next to a covered plate with a stack of blueberry pancakes was a note:

Gone to run some errands. Enjoy breakfast! See you soon. Mom.

Her mother had added a little heart to the note.

Michelle smiled to herself as she scooped a generous serving of oatmeal into a bowl, relieved to see these indications of her mother's affection, despite the abrupt end to the evening's conversation.

It wasn't long before Maya came home, warmly announcing her return as she unlocked the door. "Shelley, I'm home!"

"I'm in the living room, momma," Michelle called out.

Maya put her bible on a side table, hung up her coat, and came to join Michelle.

"Thanks for the yummy breakfast momma," Michelle said as she hugged her mom and kissed her on the cheek.

"You're welcome Shelley, it's nice to be able to cook for you again."

They sat, smiling and enjoying the warmth of the moment.

Then Maya's smile broadened.

"I've been watching you dance."

Michelle's raised her eyebrows and her eyes widened.

"You have?" Michelle's brow furrowed as she considered how this could be.

"Yes, your African dance troupe, Uhuru. I found recordings of your performances online. I was looking for something, anything, that could give me some more insight into your college experience. What a treasure to find those recordings."

Michelle sat back in her chair as she thought through the ramifications of this. Joining the troupe had been such a stretch out of her comfort zone. She had not even considered the possibility that her mom might see those performances one day. Well, she was sure glad about that. It was hard enough as it was.

Maya continued: "Oh Shelley, seeing you dance gave me a glimpse into how you were growing and stretching. Whoo, the joy and freedom you were expressing with your body, girl. And the smile on your face. Mmmm, it was like I was seeing a whole other person. And I could tell at first you were quite self-conscious. Who wouldn't be! But it was not long before I could tell that my Shelley had grown so comfortable being on that stage."

Michelle nodded and smiled, "You're right momma, I've come to really love those dance performances."

Maya's voice turned more reflective. "Seeing you dance really got me thinking. That sense of . . . liberation in your body. I wondered about what other ways you were freeing yourself to grow and learn." She shook her head. "I thought about myself. How I could not *imagine* getting up there on that stage like that. Freely expressing myself in front of all those people."

She looked at Michelle more intently now.

"I would not have thought that kind of personal transformation was possible. I figured people were either born performers, or not. You know, some people just *love* to be the center of attention. But you've always been more reserved and even a little shy. To see you liberate yourself physically like that, really opened my eyes. Whoo, I've had so many questions Shelley. Was that joy always in you waiting to get out? Had I maybe been holding you back from your true self-expression?" She paused. "Could there be something more free like that in me?"

Michelle had not anticipated this level of self-reflectiveness from her mother. She let out a long exhale, raised her eyebrows once again, and sat silently, not sure what to say.

"And then you unload all of that on me yesterday," Maya stated, crossing her arms. "Here I thought I had gotten myself ready to learn from your journey. I knew you would have some interesting self-discovery to share. But oh Shelley, what you said is so hard for me to hear. You're raising some really harsh concerns about how I prepared you to make your way in this world."

Maya paused, a sadness settled back over her for the first time this morning.

"I sense that there is truth in what you are telling me Shelley. And I certainly know you now carry that as your truth. I, I. . .I guess just don't feel ready to second guess all the ways that I have tried to do right by you."

Michelle nodded thoughtfully. "I really hear you momma. And I know this will be difficult. Honestly, part of me just wants to let it all go and avoid any risk of seeming insensitive or ungrateful. But pushing through some hard self-reflection has been crucial for the sense of freedom and confidence I now feel as a Black woman."

She eased herself up from the table. "I could use a little walk after that big breakfast. Let me get a little fresh air and then let's talk some more, ok momma?"

Maya nodded and smiled. "Sounds good Shelley, be safe out there."

***

When she returned from her walk, Michelle found her mom sitting on the living room sofa staring pensively out of the window. She sat down next to her and took her mother's hands in hers.

"I love you momma. I know you've wanted the best for me. I am not blaming you or even criticizing you. This is not your fault, this is what society has taught you. This what your mother taught you and her mother taught her."

Michelle took a deep breath and forged on.

"But I've learned that we must acknowledge and name the racism that we have internalized inside ourselves. The ways that we have come to believe deep, deep down that Black people are not as good as White people."

"But Shelley, how can you possibly say I ever did not push for the best for you?" Maya queried.

Michelle was very ready for this. "Momma, remember when I wanted to take advanced math in 8th grade instead of regular math, what did you say?"

Maya shook her head slowly, saddened by the memory. "I was so scared that you would fail, that it would be too hard for you. I did not want you to be humiliated."

Michele shook her own head in response. "And momma, why was the advanced course fine for the White students to take? Was there no chance they might fail too?"

"Shelley, I was just so worried that it was too much of a stretch for you."

"But momma, my math teacher and my guidance counselor said that they thought I could do it."

"Yes," Maya acknowledged, "but they're White, and I was not convinced they had your best interests at heart like I did." She crossed her arms and pursed her lips, indicating she was not sorry about this stance she had taken back then.

"Momma, listen to yourself!" Michelle raised her palms upward, gesturing at Maya in exasperation. "The two of them had high expectations for me, in that case it was *you* who was holding me back!" She took a breath to calm herself. "You're right that so many of my teachers did not see my full potential. But momma, I'm talking about you. For you, what was it about me that made me more vulnerable to failure than other students?"

"Well...it was..." Maya started to answer, then paused.

"Yes?" Michelle raised both eyebrows expectantly.

"Because you are..." Another pause.

"Yes? Say it momma."

"Because you are Black." Maya eyes softened as she held Michelle's gaze, a full understanding now taking hold.

Michelle pressed on. "And how did you feel about me leaving Cleveland to attend college in another city in another state?"

"I hated it." Maya stated firmly.

"Why did you hate it momma?"

Maya answered quickly, this was something she had struggled mightily with. "Because you would be so far away from me. Because I couldn't protect you. Because you would have to figure out so many unfamiliar things."

Michelle's eyes softened now too. "And momma, why was I more vulnerable to being away, to being unprotected, and to having to figure out unfamiliar things? Why momma?"

"Because you are Black." Maya's eyes drifted downwards once more. There was a long silence, but it was a comfortable, reflective moment.

Maya raised her head and looked directly into Michelle's eyes now, nodding in affirmation.

"Because you are Black," she repeated softly.

Michelle smiled with pride and satisfaction.

"I am Black, momma. And I am strong. And I am resilient. And I am capable of anything I set my mind to. And so are you. We must remove and overcome the negative self-perceptions that have been planted deep inside us by this racist society." She slowed her voice for emphasis. "This is the most dangerous form of racism. The racist beliefs about ourselves that we hold within our *own* minds. We must constantly question and counter these beliefs."

Maya stood slowly and walked over to the window. Her shoulders relaxed and her gaze seemed to be aimed well beyond the street outside.

She turned and smiled for the first time since their morning conversation. "I hear you Shelley, I really do. It is truly painful to think of myself as having played any role in holding you back. And playing any part in keeping racism alive. But you've helped me begin to see it now. I've got a lot more thinking to do about this. But you've really opened my eyes."

Now she sat and took Michelle's hands in her own.

"What a truly proud and confident Black woman you've become, Shelley my love."

She reached up, took Michelle's face in her hands, and leaned forward to kiss her forehead and then each of her cheeks.

"Thank you for helping me see this so lovingly. Thank you for loving me despite where I've fallen short."

"Oh momma," Michelle smiled through tears of appreciation, "there are so many ways you have made me all that I am. And now we can continue our journey of learning, and unlearning, together!"

"I would love that sweetheart," Maya said. "But I guess it will have to be at a distance since you'll be headed off to school again in just a few weeks," Maya sighed with the weight of sad maternal acceptance.

"Actually momma," Michelle said softly, "I'm not heading back to school next semester."

Maya caught her breath, not daring to hope that her darling daughter had decide to stay close to her. Could it be? Oh, the joys they could have together with their new understanding and closeness.

"I'm going to study abroad for my junior year."

Maya squeezed her eyes tightly shut and tried to unhear what she had just heard.

The room was completely silent once again.

Michelle sat patiently, waiting for her mother to compose herself.

Maya opened her eyes and was about to speak when her phone buzzed. She glanced at the screen. "It's my neighbor Ms. Hunt," she explained, "lemme make sure she's ok." She stood up and walked out of the room as she answered the call.

When Maya came back into the room just a few minutes later, Michelle had placed the airline ticket envelope on the coffee table.

Her heart beating fast, Maya picked it up and read the destination on the ticket.

"New Zealand!" she shrieked. She looked at Michelle incredulously. And looked back at the ticket to make sure she had read correctly. Yes, the destination was Wellington, New Zealand.

Her shoulders slumped once more.

"Oh Shelley, honey," she murmured, her eyes lifting to look pleadingly into Michelle's eyes. "But New Zealand is on the other side of the world. Why do you have to go so far?"

Michelle's eyes sparkled with intellectual intensity.

"Because that's where the Māori people are," she stated authoritatively. "One of the most resilient and well-known indigenous cultures in the world, in a moment where the colonial power is increasingly open to more fully honoring their rights. I've received a fellowship to go learn about the role of women leaders in contemporary Māori culture. I'll be working with a team of female Māori researchers."

Maya sat back in her chair, shaking her head and gazing at her daughter with a mix of wonder, pride and exasperation.

She looked down at the ticket envelope in her hand, and then raised an eyebrow, noticing for the first time that there were two airline tickets in the ticket holder, not just one.

"And just who else is going on this little adventure with you Michelle?" she couldn't help but take an accusatory tone.

Michelle's face broke into an impish grin, her eyes gleamed, and it was clear she had been waiting for this delicious moment for a long, long time.

"You are momma, you are."

Author's Reflection

The *Passenger* story was about curiosity, or a lack thereof, and also about perception and bias, the second component of my Everyday Antiracism framework. That freed me up to push deeper into the issue of perception with *Awakening*, and I was eager to tackle the sensitive topic of internalized racism among Black people.

This is the most insidious and pernicious form of racism. Over generations, White supremacy has successfully been wired into the heads of Black people. This means you could remove interpersonal, institutional and systemic racism tomorrow and yet we Black folks would still have vital work to do to cease consciously and subconsciously believing that White things - neighborhoods, schools, products, people - are inherently superior.

Given the sensitivity of the topic, I wanted a gentle space to explore it. This led me to a mother-daughter relationship at the stage where the daughter is gaining emotional and intellectual maturity and the mother may be open to learning from her.

The seed for this story was planted years ago, at a workshop on countering racism, when I witnessed a middle-aged Black woman having a transformative but devastating revelation about the so-called "White room" in her house.

I could not resist sending Michelle off to New Zealand where my own daughter headed one summer during college to conduct medical anthropology in collaboration with Māori researchers. Like Maya, my wife and I unexpectedly had our horizons greatly expanded when we got to go visit her.

How comfortable are you with the notion of "internalized racism"?

Could you explain to others why it is the most insidious and dangerous form of racism?

If you are Black, what can you do to confront your own internalized racism, and that of your family and social network?

If you are not Black, how does understanding internalized racism help you better understand the emotional tax of racism on Black people, while recognizing that this does not let you and others off the hook for addressing interpersonal, institutional and systemic racism?

Doing It Our Way

February 15

I DON'T BELONG here.

Like, I really, really DON'T BELONG here.

They don't get me. They don't WANNA get me.

They can't even CONCEIVE of someone like me.

February 16

Wow, I just kept it REAL in that entry yesterday, didn't I!

Yeah, I was feeling SUPER SHITTY.

Feeling better today. I looooooooove my social studies class. Ms. Anderson makes it so INTERESTING. And she treats us like we actually have BRAINS and can think for ourselves. Not like you just open the top of our heads and pour the information in.

I really like how she asks A LOT of questions. Like REALLY GOOD questions. She makes me THINK.

I feel like I BELONG in her class. Like she SEES me. Like, the REAL ME.

Why can't the REST of Shaker Heights High School feel like this?

February 19

Being a first-year high school student really SUCKS.

I just.

Feel.

Sad.

Sad. SAD. Sad. SAD. Sad.

February 20

Still feeling pretty SAD.

I just don't know WHERE I fit in.

EVERYONE else seems to know their thing and have their crew.

Next year HAS to be better, right? I'll start finding MY place by then, right?

February 22

I mean, I don't get it.

This is THE Shaker Heights.

All this hype about being one of the first communities in the WHOLE country to encourage white people to not run away when black people moved into their neighborhood.

Been on magazines and documentaries and news shows.

I even heard there's a new book called Dream Town by a Washington
Post writer who grew up in Shaker.

Dream Town. Oh yeah?

So WHY don't I feel included???????????

February 28

Okay, I'll say it.

Why is it still considered SO strange to not feel like a girl OR a boy?

What if I just DON'T?

I'm just me.

Billie Blackburn with some girlness and some boyness and some just
me-ness.

I'm not tall or short, I'm just me – kinda medium height.

I'm not skinny or chubby, I'm just me – kinda middly.

I'm not light-skinned or dark-skinned, I'm just me – kinda brown.

And I don't feel like a girl or a boy – I'm just me – BILLIE.

March 1

I looooooove being BLACK.

I looooooove BLACK people. We are soooooooo COOL.

The Sankofa Arts and Culture Performance this past weekend was DA
BOMB!

I am sooooo PROUD of all the students who have been working for
months to prepare the show.

What if we were truly free to revel in our BLACKNESS all the time,
not just at the Black History Month celebration????????????

Maybe next year I can work on the poster design – I just LOVE the poster they had this year! I think I could do something COOL like that!

March 12

Omigod. I cannot believe this school year is SO FAR FROM OVER!!! My first year of high school and it feels soooooooo LONG. I mean, soooooooo DAMN LONG.

There's so much I LOVE about living here in Shaker Heights and going to school here.

But there is so much I HATE. I mean really HATE.

Like I hate snakes. Ewwww. Like I hate broccoli. Yechhhh. Like I hate Instagram. Like I hate football. And lacrosse. And ice hockey. And wrestling. And boxing. And rugby. And all those violent sports where sweaty-ass guys, and some girls I guess, just love bashing into each other for fun.

And I HATE HATE HATE when some people make other people feel like they don't BELONG.

Anyway, journal, you already know what I hate. And what I love. And who I love. Or at least have a big ol' crush on. Ahhhhhhhh.

But what you don't know yet, is that I am DONE. I. Am. Done. Terminado. It's a wrap. I am soooooooo DONE.

Done with what, you ask, oh journal, dear journal?

With feeling like an OUTSIDER. With feeling like I don't belong. With the POPULAR kids running everything. Why do THEY get to dictate what's COOL and UNCOOL?

I'm not taking it ANY MORE.

Maybe it's time to do things ANOTHER WAY.
Stay tuned!

March 15

Okayyyyyy, things are MOVING.
I stayed after school today and went to talk to Ms. Anderson about my ideas for how things could be DIFFERENT and she was soooooooo encouraging!
She said I should run for Student Council President next year and make those things HAPPEN!
Can you IMAGINE?
I said that she was crazzzzzzzzy to suggest that a rising sophomore could be elected as Student Council President. Especially an OUT-SIDER like me.
And she said WHY NOT?!
In fact, better yet, she said WHY THE HELL NOT, BILLIE BLACKBURN?!?!
I looooove when adults CURSE around us teens, it feels like they are acknowledging that we are GROWING UP.
Okay, time to talk to Lisa about this!!

March 16

We are REALLY MOVING now!
Talked to my bestie Lisa Chang and guess what! She was ALL about it!
Not only that, she said SHE would run as my Vice-President!
And since she's gonna be a junior – that will bring support from her classmates TOO.

I'm soooooooo glad we met in an Art class and became besties when we decided to join Art Club together. She's artsy and creative like me, but she is a bigtime people person – she can get ANYBODY to talk to her.

I think that's why she's been such a great best friend for me – she brings out my friendliness. See Billie, she likes to say, you DO like people!

She also said she would join the Gender and Sexuality Alliance with me, as an ally. I'm gaining so much CONFIDENCE from being around those folx. And I don't think I would have had the COURAGE to join and express my identity as gender non-binary without her SUPPORT.

And Lisa had a GREAT idea. We're gonna build a slate of candidates for each of the Student Council Executive Committee roles, President, Vice-President, Secretary, Treasurer, with one student from each class year. And we figured out the next person we are doing to try to recruit.

I hope, hope, hope he says YES!

Fingers crossed!!!!!!!!!!!

March 19

We've got the next member of our slate!

It was Lisa's idea to see if we could convince Scott Williams to join us to represent next year's first-year class. He's an 8th grader and we've gotten know him through the Gender and Sexuality Alliance where he's been hanging out, as the leader of the middle school LGBTQ+ student group. He's also an incredible cross country runner and he's been training with the high school team, so he already knows sooooo many high schoolers.

He has such a dynamic personality. It's no wonder because he's got

culture and flavor on both sides - his dad is Dominican and his mom
is from New Orleans. They moved to Shaker just a couple years ago.
Oh, and there's more!
We have our campaign slogan.
WE ALL BELONG HERE.
Yessssss!
That just sounds SO GOOD!
WE ALL BELONG HERE.
Look out Shaker Heights.

March 23

Just daydreaming about Julie Edwards. Ahhhhh.
Sat near her today in Art Club and I could watch her working on her
cool-ass drawing without her seeing me staring.
She is just soooooooo CUTE.
And she is such an amazzzzzzzzing artist.
Ahhhhh, I love thinking about her and me walking, holding hands,
and just talking for hours and hours and hours and hours.

April 10

Whew! So MUCH happening. Hard to keep up with journaling.
Student Council campaigning has REALLY ramped up.
We have some strong competition, but, check this out, my biggest
competitor HAS JOINED OUR SLATE!
Yup! Erin Baratz, the STAR soccer player and BIG theater personality,
looked like she could be a LOCK to be elected as the next Student
Council President. She is the current Vice-President and usually that's
an EASY stepping stone to the next level.

But then we unveiled our WE ALL BELONG HERE pitch.

Scott had the brilliant idea to kick off the campaign with a HAVE IT YOUR WAY smoothie bar.

We talked it over with the administration and you wouldn't believe, or maybe you would, all the hurdles.

What if some students can afford what you are selling and some can't?

What will be the smoothie ingredients?

Will it be sanitary?

What about allergies?

We figured out how to make it happen: our parents all chipped into make it a free giveaway, we picked ingredients that were all within state nutritional guidelines, and each student would make their smoothie themselves.

Idea approved!!!

We set up a table in the cafeteria and created a colorful display. We had a big poster that said:

FREE MAKE-YOUR-OWN SMOOTHIES

FROM

BILLIE BLACKBURN, LISA CHANG AND SCOTT WILLIAMS

FOR STUDENT COUNCIL

WE ALL BELONG HERE

NO MATTER HOW YOU LIKE YOUR SMOOTHIE!

And we had ALL KINDS of smoothie ingredients: fruit, yogurt, and all different kinds of milk – regular milk, skim milk, soy milk, oat milk, rice milk.

Our table looked soooooooo COLORFUL with all that fruit! And boy was it a hit! And everyone was talking about the way THEY liked THEIR smoothie. Even the people who HATE smoothies got in the

conversation about why they DON'T like smoothies.
Something for everyone! We all belong!

April 11

Oops – forgot to finish the part about Erin Baratz!
Once she saw our CREATIVITY and our MISSION displayed in its
full glory with our kickoff campaign, she asked to speak to me after
school.
I almost peed my pants when she asked if SHE could join OUR
candidate slate as OUR SECRETARY!
I said I needed to check with Lisa and Scott, but I just KNEW they
were going to say YES. Are you KIDDING me? One of the most
WELL-KNOWN juniors in the school? Who also turns out to be an
ALLY OF OUR CAUSE!? Omigod, right???????
We are rolling!!!!!!

May 5

We won! We won! We won!
Once Erin joined us, the other candidates really didn't have a chance!
Now we get to do this OUR WAY!
We've got to FOCUS on our final exams and papers for now. And then
we've got the summer to plan for A NEW DAY IN SHAKER.

May 28

So, I'm in love. Gotta go! She's calling me now!

May 29

So, remember that big ol' secret crush I had?

Would you believe she's been crushin' for me too???

Julie. Edwards.

Her lovely Julie-ness.

She's a sophomore too. And she's an artsy type like me – she is an incredible graphic artist.

She is sooooooo CUTE. And soooooo SMART.

And she has STRONG opinions and is not afraid to speak her mind.

I guess she thought I might be a little too QUIET and MEEK for her. But when she saw me step out and campaign for Student Council President, she said she KNEW we could be a great match.

And now I can't stop thinking about her.

August 4

Wow this summer has FLOWN by!

Between lots and lots of time with my sweet Julie, my job at Mitchell's Ice Cream, bestie time with Lisa and some vacation time with family, there hasn't been time for much else.

Lisa, Scott, Erin and I have our first meeting tomorrow to start making plans for the Student Council.

I've got a few big ideas to run by them. If we're doing this BELONG-ING thing, we gotta be ALL ABOUT it! Business as usual is OVER!

First, we gotta change the NAME of this thing.

The Student Council could now be the Student Stewards.

We are the Stewards of a new vibe at Shaker Heights High.

A BELONGING vibe.

Our role is to envision it, name it, model it and nourish it.

And our Executive Committee could now be renamed the Guiding Stewards.

Our first priority should be to make sure that EVERY SINGLE first-year student feels welcome from Day One.

We'll start by assigning each first-year a MENTOR from a higher grade.

The mentors can be optional, no one will be FORCED to have one.

But, at a minimum, every single first-year student will get a FRIEND-LY call from older student saying "Welcome to Shaker Heights High School, where EVERY STUDENT belongs. Is there anything we can do to help support a great start for you this year?"

Can't wait to see what the crew thinks of my ideas!

August 6

Yayyyyyy. Our new Guiding Stewards team is off to a great start!

Since I can get discounts for us at Mitchell's Ice Cream, we've decided we MUST MUST MUST hold our summer meetings there. How can you not have a GOOD meeting while eating ICE CREAM??????

They liked my ideas and we turned our focus on how to have a first day of school that was like NONE OTHER. That would give our Belonging Campaign a ROCKET BOOST.

We asked ourselves: what would help students feel a real sense of BELONGING?

We realized there are TWO ways to feel ENGAGED and CON-NECTED in a place.

One is to do things that YOU LIKE with other people who SHARE YOUR INTERESTS.

Another way is to try out NEW THINGS and make NEW CON-

NECTIONS with people.

So we're going to propose a FESTIVAL DAY to kick off the school year, to replace the usual first day of class.

Here's what we're thinking!!!!!

It will be a fun festival with all kinds of cool activities and games – some REALLY ACTIVE and some REALLY CHILL.

For the FIRST HALF of the day students will get to choose activities that are familiar to them, likely with people that they know. This will feel like a FUN REUNION after the long summer.

For the SECOND HALF of the day everyone will be encouraged to try some NEW ACTIVITIES and meet some NEW PEOPLE.

I sure hope the administration LIKES it – it's kind of a crazzzzzzyyyyy idea – but would be soooooooooo cool!

August 14

Woah. So is this what happens behind the scenes of this leadership stuff ALL THE TIME??????

So first, our principal, Dr. Stella Richardson, LOVED our back-to-school FESTIVAL DAY idea. She's in just her second year as principal, she came here from Detroit where she had been a principal for years. And she told us she is REALLY READY to try some new stuff! Yayyyy.

And the assistant principal, Ms. Johnson, HATED IT.

"Think of all the LOGISTICS" she said.

"We're pushing back everything by a WHOLE DAY" she said.

"What if somebody gets HURT?" she said.

And then, Dr. Richardson asked us to step outside while she and Ms. Johnson talked it out.

When we came back into the room, Dr. Richardson told us that our idea WAS APPROVED!

And all the while Ms. Johnson was sitting over on the side looking MADDDDDDDD.

Ummmm, awkward!

Well, we're ready to convene the whole Student Stewards group and get to work planning the Festival!

September 12

Whoooo it's been a BUSY, BUSY start to the year.

I really like a couple of my classes A LOT, and the other ones pretty much seem like they WON'T be the worst. Well Biology seems like it's gonna really SUCK the whole way, but overall, NOT bad!

And I've met sooooooo many new people in my new stewardship role and best of all soooo many people seem to be enjoying our new BELONGING vibe!

Ok, gotta back up, so much to tell.

So the Festival went GREAT! Great, great, great, great, great! Just SO GREAT.

Starting the day with familiar activities was a super good idea because everyone was in their COMFORT ZONE, the quiet kids could do quiet stuff, the nerd kids could nerd out, we artsy folks got all artsy, and the active kids could work off that active energy. But then the best part was when everyone was trying something NEW and meeting NEW PEOPLE.

In that moment Shaker Heights felt.....DIFFERENT. Like we were creating a new kinda SPACE together. A space for EVERYONE.

Lisa had the fabulous idea to set up a HELP US DESIGN OUR BELONGING VIBE table to collect ideas from students about other ways to promote belonging at the school.

Man, oh man, we got suchhhhhhhhh great ideas! We had a BLAST at our next Student Stewards meeting sorting through the ideas and selecting the ones we are going to roll out this fall.
Check THESE out!

- Rotating student welcome greeters at each doorway at the beginning of each day of school

- A Belonging Suggestion Box in the front office where students can put anonymous ideas about something that would help them feel more welcome at the school

- A Belonging Suggestion Box in each classroom where students can share ideas about that particular class

- A rotating list of quotes about belonging read over the loudspeaker every Monday morning

Erin and Scott immediately began collecting some great ones, like:

- "This is the most precious gift true love offers - the experience of knowing we always belong." bell hooks

- "A person with ubuntu is open and available to others, affirming of others, does not feel threatened that others are able and good, for he or she has a proper self-assurance that comes from knowing that he or she belongs in a greater whole and is diminished when others are humiliated or diminished." Desmond Tutu

- "Because true belonging only happens when we present our authentic, imperfect selves to the world, our sense of belonging can never be greater than our level of self-acceptance."

Brené Brown

Oh, here's one of my favorites!

- A Mash-Up After School Day once a month where different student clubs hold joint activities and different sports teams have a fun practice together – like Art Club and Robotics Club doing an activity together or like the soccer team and field hockey team sharing a workout.

And you wouldn't believe how many kids have been stopping me in the hallway to share other ideas!

Oh what fun!

September 28

Oh what a pain in the ass!

Dealing with the HATERS. Omigod. Really?!?!

So me, Lisa, Scott and Erin got invited to a conversation with the High School Parent-Teacher Organization Co-Chairs.

Thinking it was gonna be a FUN conversation, we suggested we meet at Mitchells. I can't believe we invited them into OUR special meeting spot.

And here we are thinking that they would be bringing some ideas of their own, and asking about how they could SUPPORT us.

Oh no, no, no. Not EVEN close.

There we were sitting with our ice cream all MELTING as they proceed to tell us how these belonging activities have gotten "way out of hand."

Can you believe this shit?

I was sooooooo mad, I couldn't even really hear what they were trying to say. Lisa had to fill me in later.

I guess it's something about the "pace of change." Like, they are cool with us trying some new things. But ALL these things ALL at once, is apparently not "THE SHAKER WAY."

Now what the hell is THE SHAKER WAY?!?!

I guess it's the SLOWER WAY.

The DO IT THEIR WAY WAY.

Aw, hell no. I just walked out.

And I'm gonna walk straight into Dr. Richardson's office tomorrow morning.

September 29

God bless you Dr. Richardson!!!!!!! That is the homie, for real!!!

She was so upset that the PTO Co-Chairs had tried to slow our roll, she called them right then and there while I was sitting in her office and she left voicemails for both of them.

This might get a little messy, but at least we know she has our back.

October 18

I'm so sad.

October 19

I'm still too sad to write about it.

October 20

Julie broke up with me.
Life sucks.

October 30

Soooooo....who knew changemaking could be so damn COMPLI-
CATED?
We got PAST the resistance of the Assistant Principal.
We got PAST the resistance of the PTO.
Only to have an anti-woke campaign emerge AGAINST us!
Yes. Right HERE in Shaker Heights. Nationally renowned for inclu-
sion and tolerance.
And yet some students start to CRITICIZE us for being overly woke
and forcing our wokeness on everyone. Making everyone part of some
big ol' woke experiment.
And guess who was the ringleader?
Yup, Julie. MY Julie. My sweet Julie. USED to be sweet Julie.
At first she just started acting weirder and weirder. Being kinda DIS-
TANT. Asking strange questions about the belonging activities.
Then next thing I know, she's telling me all the belonging stuff is
making her UNCOMFORTABLE. And that she knows she's not the
only one.
She said maybe not everyone wants to belong.
Huh?!?!!? Now that's some crazzzzy talk. Who DOESN'T want to feel
like they belong?????
And she said she couldn't be with me if I didn't understand her.
Well, I don't understand her.
So I guess that's it.

November 10

So here's the cool thing.

That was it for me and Julie. But thanks to my BRILLIANT Guiding Stewards team, it was actually a chance to make our belonging movement EVEN STRONGER.

Julie formed her little anti-woke group and they started their own display table at lunchtime - We Think For Ourselves, We Don't Need You To Think For us.

So Lisa, Scott, Erin and I huddled to strategize.

Scott had yet another a BRILLIANT idea (whoo that guy is sharp!). He reminded us of the make-your-own smoothie activity, and how EVEN the people who HATED smoothies were still part of the buzz around the smoothie-making.

If we truly believe that EVERYONE BELONGS, then EVEN those who want nothing to do with a belonging effort, should still feel VALUED and WELCOME.

And actually, we don't think that belonging and thinking for yourself are MUTUALLY EXCLUSIVE.

So we FLIPPED the script on Julie and the self-thinkers.

We suggested to Dr. Richardson that they be allowed to read a quote over the loudspeaker every Tuesday morning about THINKING FOR YOURSELF.

And we invited their anti-woke group to JOIN the once-a-month Afterschool Mash-Up Day and engage with whichever other group they wanted. Me and Erin thought there was NO WAY they would be interested. But Lisa and Scott were right – the anti-wokers were up for MASH-Ups and wanted to start with a joint competition with the Chess Club. Who knew!?

And we appointed a rotating Think-For-Yourself Advocate at each Student Stewards meeting whose job it is to push back and check the rest of us if we are being overly PUSHY or INTRUSIVE in our belonging activities.

Even Julie sent me a note saying that she NEVER expected to feel so welcomed and appreciated for advancing an idea in OPPOSITION to the mainstream.

We're back on track people!

Maybe it is possible to create a community where everyone feels truly and honestly like they BELONG.

***

Twelve years later...

June 19

Just found my old journal. Wow.

A walk down memory lane of the mind of 16-year-old Billie Blackburn.

And what a sophomore year that was.

I'm back in Shaker Heights for our ten-year reunion and going through some of my old things in my parents' house.

I've always told people that that was the year that everything changed for me, I'd forgotten I have this journal that details exactly why. And how.

By the way, why did I have such a thing for CAPITAL LETTERS???

And I've forgotten just how sad and lonely I felt as a first-year student, because of how deeply I found my purpose and my place after we started that Belonging Campaign.

It's so great that the Student Council is still called the Student Stewards! And so many of our practices are still happening — the mentors, the greeters, the quotes, even the Mash-Up Days.

And there are some really creative new belonging activities. My favorite is that a few years after we graduated, the seniors decided to give up the Senior Lounge and make it into Everyone's Lounge. Imagine that!

And I love seeing what Dr. Richardson has done since she was appointed Superintendent four years ago. She has taken our belonging efforts into all of the Shaker Schools, even including pre-K programs! There's still a long way to go for Shaker to be the truly inclusive environment we all know it could be, but I know Dr. Richardson will make some great progress.

Even with everything I've been able to experience since high school — college at Spelman and the Belonging Campaign we launched there, Peace Corps in Burkina Faso and the street youth network we created in Ouagadougou, international affairs graduate studies at Georgetown, and now my program associate position at the Institute for Peace in D.C. — my proudest achievement has been the belonging work in Shaker.

Lisa, Scott and Erin say the same thing about what that year meant to them. They all happen to be back in Shaker this weekend as well. And each of us can trace our current careers to our year working together as Guiding Stewards. Lisa is back living in Shaker and is the Director for Student Engagement and Inclusion at the High School. Scott is working as Assistant Director for Trusted Space Partners doing community network-building, he just opened an office location for them in Durham, NC. And Erin is the Director of Public Relations for Partners in Health, based in Haiti.

And Julie Edwards?

Well, stay tuned. Julie and I are going to meet up for a drink tonight. She reached out when she heard I was in town.

I'm excited to see her.

Ah, it's good to be back in Shaker.

And to feel like I BELONG here. :)

Author's Reflection

The idea for this story started with me wanting to write at least one of the stories in this volume in the first-person narrative voice (*Divine Restitution* takes it one step further with an omniscient first-person narrator). Changing the narrative!

As I reflected on the components of the Everyday Antiracism framework, Belonging seemed like a great one to explore from the perspective of the person who was being excluded. And then I had to decide who the character would be, and in what setting. I think the notion of a teenager in a high school setting came pretty quickly, as a time when many of us - all of us? - struggle with a sense of not fitting in in some way.

Once I had the high school focus – it was clear that I would set the story in Shaker Heights, Ohio where all three of my children went through most of their schooling, and where my wife and I created and led a parent-community advocacy group called ONE Shaker to advance strategies to eliminate the racial achievement gap (the book *Dream Town: The Quest for Racial Equity in Shaker Heights* is a recent comprehensive history of 100 years of racism and antiracism in Shaker). The barriers that Billie and the other students encounter from the school administration, the Parent-Teachers Organization, and their peers reflect our own experiences.

Ok, so then who would the protagonist be within Shaker Heights High School? To stretch my own exploration of exclusion and be- longing, I leaned toward a female student, and then leaned further from my own familiarity to center a gender non-binary student. I hope I've captured their voice and experience with as much empathy and humanity as someone who has not walked that path can. Billie

Blackburn is named, as are most of my characters, with reference to individuals from along my life journey. In this case, it was an opportunity to recognize the two leaders of Trusted Space Partners, the organization referenced late in the story, which is an actual community network-building consulting organization based in North Carolina. The founders, Frankie Blackburn and Bill Traynor are two beloved friends, mentors, and close colleagues of many years from whom I've learned much of what I know about promoting belonging through intentional practice. This story is a love and appreciation letter to both of them as well as a manifesto transmitting their wisdom to all of you.

There are so many delightful and simple ways to create spaces and experiences that cultivate a sense of belonging if we just give ourselves permission to be proactive, intentional, human-centered, and creative.

It was a joy to let my own imagination soar about how Billie and their allies would do things THEIR way at Shaker Heights High School.

How might you apply a little more creativity and imagination to the spaces you have influence in shaping?

Who might currently not feel a full sense of belonging in those spaces?

How can you push through the inevitable resistance when you and your collaborators attempt to do things a different way?

And The Truth Will
Get You, Freed

Y ou have never felt better.

You leap out of your Tesla Model X.

You toss your keys to the valet and give him a wink.

Despite the gloomy rain clouds overhead, you feel lighthearted.

You stride confidently up the front walkway of the country club, shoulders back and chin slightly raised.

Your pace is brisk as if there is a special wind at your back.

You are smiling, as if you are living a life in which there is always something to smile about.

A porter opens the door for you. Something about the gesture feels so right and so familiar. The path ahead opening up before you, as usual.

You see your classmate Thomas Johnson coming out of the club as you enter. You avoid catching his eye because you feel sorry for him. It's not your fault he never won a match against you in the state tennis tournament.

Becky Stockridge is in the lounge reading as you walk by. You pretend not to notice that she has put down her book to gaze at you longingly. Leave 'em wanting more, you purr to yourself.

Your phone buzzes with an alert. You glance at it to see a bank notification that a deposit has posted and the fabulous nine-figure balance in that account has ticked up slightly.

Ah, life is great.

***

"Good afternoon, Mr. Freed." The maître d' greets you warmly, but without his usual flair. "Your parents are already here, let me show you where they are sitting."

He turns to an associate, "Mr. Pierce Freed is here to dine with his parents, please manage the front while I escort him to his table."

You walk along behind him as he weaves among the restaurant tables. You note that his movements are stiffer than usual. His neck and shoulders seem tense. Normally, he checks on the diners as he passes, but today he seems intent on getting you to your destination as soon as possible.

As you reach the table where your parents are sitting, two things make clear that something is amiss. The maître d' does not acknowledge your parents but turns brusquely to walk away. And there are strained looks on your parents' faces. If they had already been served their food, you might have thought that they had both taken a bite of something distasteful.

Your mother's anxiety is plain to see. Karen Freed is a deeply kind human being, the type who opens a window and spends a half hour shooing a fly outside to safety, rather than grabbing for the fly swatter. Though never having worked a paying job in her life, she fills every day with activity—volunteer commitments, book clubs, arts and cultural events—and, of course, making sure you have everything you need. She dresses fashionably but sensibly, with attractive but unpretentious jewelry. Normally, her amiable oval face is flushed pink and quick to smile. But now her face is drained of color and worry lines form waves on her forehead. You get the sense that if she could leap up, wrap you in her arms, and shield you from whatever bad news they are about to lay on you, she would in a heartbeat. You try to remember when last, if ever, you have seen her looking so worried.

Your dad is harder to read. Dick Freed has made a career of being the inscrutable guy in the room. An investment fund manager just like you, but at a stratospheric scale of wealth. Everything about him—his carefully coiffed hair, well-tailored suit, cuff links and gold watch—exudes privilege, power and poise. An avid poker player, he has won many a round with absolutely nothing of value in his hand, but with a steely-eyed confidence that intimidated others into folding prematurely. Most observers would see that same poise in place today. But you see signs of anxiety. His eyes are narrowed, his jaw is clenched, and his shoulders are raised ever so slightly.

"Mom, dad, what's wrong?" you ask, pulling up a seat at the table and taking a sip of water to ease your suddenly very dry throat.

There is a long uncomfortable pause as they both stare at you. Is that pity that you see in their eyes?

You are suddenly overwhelmed by dread that after this moment, nothing will ever be the same.

"Is everyone okay?" you stammer, "Did something happen to nana? To grandpa?"

"No, son," your dad finally speaks. "It's us. It's you. It's everything."

Your mom drops her head and stares into her lap. Is she quietly sobbing?

"Dad, you are freaking me out, what is going on?" you demand, a bead of cold sweat working its way down the side of your face.

"Son, it's all over and we gotta come clean with you. And this is gonna be really tough."

Your mom lifts her head and looks imploringly into your eyes. "Sweetie, please know that you are our precious, precious boy and everything we've done has been because we love you and want the best for you."

"Okaayyyy..." you respond, "what exactly have you done?"

"Too much," your mother sighs, "way too much." Her eyes go back to her lap.

"Dad?!?" You turn to him, your arms stretched to the side, palms facing up. "What *is* the deal here?"

He takes a long, deep breath. And then exhales. "My companies are under investigation for fraud. All of them. And the government has frozen all our assets."

"Oh my God. Oh my God." You lean back in your chair taking in the weight of all this. "It's okay dad, we'll get through this, I can cover us with my company."

"Pierce, your company's assets are frozen too."

You feel ice in your veins.

"But, but, how can that be? How dare they! We will fight this, we will prove them all wrong!"

"Son," your father's eyes look sadder than you have ever seen them. "They are completely right. There is no fight here."

"No fight!?! But you've been working all your life to build all of this!" you protest.

"And it's all been a lie." He seems to be aging before your eyes.

"Huh? A lie? Dad, how much of it?" you manage to croak.

"All of it, son. All of it."

Your father begins to recount the situation. His investment fund business, the early successes, the difficult times, the development of a Ponzi scheme that seemed ironclad, the change in federal investment policy, the efforts to hide the scheme under increasing layers of obfuscation, and ultimately, this morning, the delivery of a federal indictment and the freezing of all his accounts. And all of yours too.

"Wait, why mine?" you snap out of your daze and remember that your company is completely independent from your father's. Why would your financial assets get caught up with his illegal activity?

"I built my company myself. I run my company myself. I'm my own man!" you object.

Your dad shakes his head sadly, and glances at your mom, who does the same.

"Son. No, you didn't. No, you don't. And no, you aren't."

"I *didn't* build my company myself? I *don't* run my company myself? And I'm *not* my own man?" you repeat, to make sure you are hearing him correctly. "Dad, what the hell are you talking about?"

He clears his throat.

"You actually don't run your company, I do. Oh, you certainly go to work every day, and you meet with clients, and you make business decisions. But that is all a shadow outfit I created to keep you busy and happy. No way I could trust you with real money and a real business."

"But I went out and raised my own capital to start the company," you counter, "I explicitly did not want to rely on your assistance, so I went to our neighbor, Mr. Franklin, the banker, and I arranged a personal loan from him."

"And he came to me," your dad replies, "and I gave him the money to loan to you."

"And, and, all the employees of my company? And all the, the clients I meet with?" you stammer.

"All paid actors," he replies.

"Get the fuck outta here dad, no way!!" You leap to your feet, knocking over your water glass. "Mom!?" You look to her to save you from this surreal nightmare unfolding around you. She looks back at you sadly and nods her head, as she sets the glass upright and uses her napkin to dab at the spilled water. This madness is true.

You sit back down.

"But dad, mom, I made the decision to skip getting an MBA, because I was so ready to run a company. You all supported my decision because you said I did not need business school."

"Actually Pierce," your mom explains, "we wanted you to go to business school, but you did not get into any of the ten you applied to."

"Huh? Mom – I *never* applied to any schools, remember?" you correct her.

"My dear, you actually did, it's you who don't remember," she asserts.

Now you are thoroughly confused. "What? How would I not remember something I did?"

She continues, "you know that therapist you've been seeing for a few years now?"

"Yeahhh..." you reply, drawing out the word, there was always something strange about that guy, with his deep, calming voice and his slow-motion movements.

"He's actually a hypnotist, not a therapist. He's helped us . . .shape your world in a way that would maintain your happiness." Her eyes are pleading now, wanting you to see that this was all for your own good.

"Shape my wor--? Maintain my happ-? What the hell are you telling me?" The house of cards that is Pierce Freed's life of success is slowly tumbling before your very eyes.

"But I did get myself into Harvard for undergrad, right? I mean, that was real, yes?"

"You got yourself onto the waiting list," your dad says, "and a well-timed anonymous gift, well, anonymous to the public, got you right off that list and into the class of 2015."

"Well how about the state essay contest I won, I remember writing every word of that essay!" you protest.

"Oh, you sure did dear," your mom agrees, "but that's not the essay that was submitted. We paid a writer to put something better together."

You're absolutely dumbfounded. Is nothing real? You perk up. "Tennis!" you state with welcome certainty. "I played *every one* of those matches myself."

Your dad nods. "Oh yes, you played every match yourself. But for the crucial ones, we made sure the umpires had a little incentive to help with key calls. And, your frequent opponent, Thomas Johnson, our little side payments for him to throw his matches against you covered at least a year of his college tuition."

You're starting to get the full picture. "And our debate team championship?" you ask hesitantly.

"Didn't you find it odd how many of the other team's members called off sick the day of the finals?" your dad asks.

Your phone buzzes. You check and see that it's your best friend Dale Stephens. Ah Dale. Your guy. Warm relief floods over you. Just like him to know when to call. You can't wait to hear what he makes of all this. He'll know how to help you feel better.

If there's anyone more self-assured than you, it's Dale. But his confidence and can-do spirit has come without all the trappings of wealth that you've enjoyed. One of the few African Americans in your elementary school, middle school and high school, Dale has been your best friend for as long as you can remember.

"I gotta take this call from Dale," you tell your parents, as you stand up.

"Errrr, about Dale..." your dad says, his voice trailing off.

You sit back down, that ice in your veins has returned.

"What about Dale?!" you practically yell, "Mom, dad, don't do this to me! Dale has been like a big brother to me."

"He *is* your big brother."

Your dad's face is deadly serious. "Dale came along from an, ah, indiscretion I had when your mom and I were engaged but not yet married. She was kind enough to forgive me and we have always supported Dale's mom. Dale does not know either, but his mom has always encouraged him to look out for you, knowing that there would be a certain bond between you two."

"So I'm not your only child!? I'm not your only special one? I'm a little brother?" The final pillar of your self-identity has been toppled.

"So, what now?" you ask dejectedly. "How are we going to handle this?"

"Pierce, there is no we, and will be no we for a long, long time." You now see remorse in your dad's eyes. "Your mom and I will be serving a long prison sentence, and you will have to figure out how to move on."

You sit back in your chair, totally defeated. "So what happens next?"

"We are no longer members at this club," your dad explains, "they were kind enough to let us have this last lunch with you." He looks at his watch. "Your mother and I will be heading to the federal building from here to turn ourselves in."

You check your own watch. "Well, I need to go for a long drive to clear my head and begin to figure out my own next steps."

Your dad shakes his head. "Pierce, because the Tesla is a company car, it has been seized."

"But my house keys were on the car ring," you respond.

"You can get them from the valet."

"And how I am supposed to get home?"

"There is a bus stop on the corner."

***

Oh, life sucks.

Your phone buzzes with an alert. You glance at it to see a bank notification that you now have zero funds available.

Becky Stockridge is still reading in the lounge when you walk by. She ignores you.

You see Thomas Johnson coming back into the club as you leave. You avoid catching his eye because you feel sorry for yourself. It's totally your fault he never won a match in the state tennis tournament.

No one opens the door for you.

You are frowning, as if life will now only give you things to frown about.

Your pace is quite slow as if there is a wind pushing against you.

You trudge forlornly down the walkway of the country club, shoulders slouched, chin to your chest.

Despite the cloudless blue sky, you feel heavyhearted.

You snatch your house keys from the valet, giving him a glare.

You walk down to the corner to catch the bus.

You have never felt worse.

Author's Reflection

Okay, let me quickly admit that I had far too much glee writing this take-down story.

It was fun to write something that is basically satire.

Presented with the opportunity to delve into the theme of Truth, I knew I would want to force a White male character to face up to some hard truths about his privilege.

And what a great opportunity to write a story in a second-person narrative voice. This gave me as narrator full control to shine the bright spotlight on the character and directly engineer each step of his unraveling.

The pyramid structure of the beginning and ending sections was the first story element to emerge as I was outlining and writing it. I actually wrote those sections from the "outside in." First sentence, inverse last sentence. Second sentence, inverse second-to-last sentence. And so on. Having laid out the symmetrical initial rise and ultimate fall of our protagonist, I could then relish the revelation of how it all fell apart for Pierce Freed.

While the story is admittedly over-dramatized, it reflects many real-world stories of falls from grace of fraudulent corporate titans. And it paints a picture of the very real layers of racial and class privilege in our society. More importantly, I hope it causes each of us to consider the "truth" of our successes and achievements. What privileges do we take for granted without noting how much of our lives is shaped by twists of fate and opportunity structures well beyond our control?

What do you think happens next for Pierce Freed? What do you think *should* happen?

Can there be redemption for those who recognize long-ignored truths and take steps to relinquish privilege?

What truths in our own lives have we not faced up to?

What are the privileges that you should be more cognizant of?

How can we interrogate our assumptions about others who have not had the same privileges we have?

The Healing

"I will BREAK THIS DOOR DOWN, you know I will!"

The heavily muscled, bald Black man laying face down on his kitchen floor twitched to consciousness at the incessant pounding on his apartment door.

"Huff! I KNOW you are in there. Goddammit, open this fucking door!" John Dolan continued to bang on the door. Short and stocky, with a grizzly red-brown beard that covered most of his ruddy face, his moist eyes conveyed the anguish he felt. His arms began to tire from his assault on the door, though he was as well-built as his prone friend inside the apartment. "Aw Huff, man, Jesus, please open this door," he implored. He backed away until he reached the wall behind him and slid down to a seated position, knees bent and head in his hands.

What if this was finally the moment that inner demons had overcome his friend? He had always feared that it would come to this. After all they had been through together, all the close calls, all the heartbreak, all the triumph, all the glimmers of hope. And from the moment they met years ago, enlisting on the same day in the same army recruitment office in Fort Worth, Texas, there had been an unusually tight bond between them. Other members of their platoon had found it hard to believe that the two of them had never previously met.

Deep down he had always worried that his good buddy would not be able to sustain his inner war. Though Richard Huffman was the strongest motherfucker he had ever met, the layers and layers of trauma and pain were more than John could imagine anyone enduring forever. "Oh Huff. I love you man," he moaned into his hands, "I'm so, so, so sorry."

"Why are YOU sorry?" Huff leaned heavily against the doorframe as he pulled the door open and looked down at his friend, crumpled on the hallway floor. "I'm the one got you out here reading my last rites, whimpering like a baby, 'cause I drank four too many, once again." He stretched out a hand to help his friend to his feet. "My bad, JD, I know I really scared you this time."

John was staring at his friend as if he wanted to make sure he was really there in front of him. But there he stood, alive and well, all six foot two of him, rubbing his chestnut brown, smooth scalp and looking back at JD with bloodshot eyes. JD wrapped Huff in a bear hug. "Oh fuck Huff, man I really thought this was it." He breathed out a long sigh. "Oh thank you God, thank you for sparing my friend." He held Huff by both shoulders and looked into his eyes. "Man, you sounded SO broken on the phone. Like you could not go on." He closed his eyes. "Oh sweet Jesus, I just knew this was it."

The two men staggered into Huff's apartment, Huff still groggy and making his way back to full consciousness and JD fatigued by the emotional strain of the evening. They each fell into chairs in the living room. Neither of them spoke for several minutes.

Finally, JD broke the silence. "Huff. You can't keep doing this to yourself. I can't go on like this either. You gotta get yourself some help."

Huff turned to look compassionately at his friend. "JD. C'mon man. You know better than anyone how hard I've tried. Shiiiiit, down at the VA they don't even ask to see my VA card any more. That cutie receptionist, the one always asking about you, SHE even calls me Huff now, instead of Mr. Huffman!" He shook his head and chuckled. "Imagine that, only motherfuckas who call me that are you, the guys from our platoon, and a perky li'l redhead at the Oakland VA."

Huff hoisted himself out of his chair with a grunt, lumbered over to the kitchen, and poured himself a glass of water. He grabbed two Red Stripes from the fridge and handed them both to JD. JD drained the first one in a long guzzle as Huff knew he would, belched loudly, and took a first gulp out of the second one. Huff sat and took a long drink of water.

"I'm all talked out dude," he stated matter-of-factly. "Those psychiatrists at the VA have probed it all out of me, man. My old man beating out his own trauma on me, my brothers and my mom. Coming and going in our lives just enough to keep us in a constant state of instability and fear. The violence in my neighborhood growing up. Seen so much death. Lost more brothers in East Oakland than in our two tours in Iraq, bro."

JD had heard all this before, numerous times, but as usual he felt useful as a compassionate, listening ear for Huff's litany of pain and loss. "It ain't right, Huff, you got a raw, raw, deal man."

"C'mon JD, you know better than that." Huff jabbed a finger accusingly at his friend. "Yeah, it ain't right. Yeah, I got a raw deal. But my WHOLE people got a raw, fuckin' deal. It ain't just me."

He sat up straighter, a moment of insight hitting him. "You know, that's the thing JD. Those VA shrinks are talking to me, probing me, trying to heal me, a sole individual," he stretched his hands out wide, palms upward, "when they are actually trying to heal my WHOLE damn ancestry and everything that's been done to us." He drained the rest of his glass. "I'm just the broken fuck at the bottom of the trauma tower, holding all the weight that The Man can pile on."

JD took another gulp from his Red Stripe. "No doubt Huff. Your people have been wronged. You have been wronged. But, bro, you are like a damn trauma junkie. No one made you enlist. No one made you demand to be sent to Iraq. No one made you volunteer for IED-clearing duty. You've been living out a death wish since you left high school."

Huff scoffed. "My death wish started long before that, my guy. Ever since I watched my youngest brother die in my arms, wishing I could have done more to keep him out of that gang life..." his voice trailed off and he closed his eyes.

His eyes flicked back open and he leaned forward looking intently at JD. "But that death wish worked out for you, didn't it my man?"

JD knew this was coming. And it was totally fair. Only reason he was sitting here now was that Huff had disobeyed orders and ran into an enemy ambush in order to retrieve JD who had been wounded and was stranded helpless and resigned to his fate. Huff had dragged JD to safety while keeping the enemy combatants at bay long enough for reinforcements to arrive and repel the attack.

"Anyway man," Huff broke the silence. "Thanks for getting up in the middle of the night and coming to check on my drunk ass."

"Bro, you know I was up anyway," JD responded, "you know me and sleep ain't the best of friends."

"Yeah, you and your insomnia," Huff nodded, "Kinda crazy for a dude as chill as you, with all that white privilege and shit, not being able to sleep through the night."

"Just one of those things, I guess," JD stated with a shrug of his shoulders. "Been that way as long as I can remember. Way before my time in the army, so I know it wasn't that. Just not the sleeping type, I guess." He stood, took his two beer bottles into the kitchen, and then walked over to give Huff a fist bump before heading toward the door. "Ok man, I'm outta here. Lemme see if I can get myself a couple hours of shut-eye before the sun comes up."

He opened the door and then turned back toward Huff. "Hey man, I was planning to hit this cultural festival happening at Lake Merritt tomorrow afternoon, how about you meet me there?"

Huff hesitated, looked like he was about to decline, and then seemed to think better of it. "Sure JD, it's the least I can do after giving you a scare tonight. I'll see you there bro."

***

It was a gorgeous summer afternoon, perfect for the annual Cultural Discovery Festival at Lake Merritt, one of Oakland's most scenic spots for leisure and recreation, just a short walk from downtown. The renowned Bay Area fog that had hovered over the city for much of the morning had burned off completely by noon, replaced by a dazzling blue sky that even the bravest of clouds dared not trespass. A pulsing reggae beat boomed hypnotically over the crowd courtesy of the energetic band prancing on the amphitheater stage.

JD and Huff strolled languidly around the festival grounds, pausing now and then to peruse a stall or exhibit that caught their attention.

Huff sipped from a whisky flask camouflaged in a small, brown paper bag. JD munched happily on a bag of kettle corn.

They browsed the jewelry and sculptures displayed outside a stall decorated to look like it was in an African market. Seeing no one minding the store, they turned to continue their meandering.

Suddenly a soft voice behind them stopped them in their tracks.

"Such pain you are carrying."

They spun around to find themselves face to face with an older Black man with a big bushy, white beard, dressed in bright, multicolored African garb.

JD spoke first, his eyes wide with surprise. "What did you say?"

"Such pain you are carrying,'" the old man repeated gently. His dark brown eyes projected utter kindness and empathy. "I'm sorry if I startled you, my friend. It's been a long time since I've seen such an emotional burden carried by such a pure heart."

The man's directness and warmth were completely disarming. JD and Huff exchanged amazed glances and seemed rooted where they stood. Though clearly stunned, neither appeared at all perturbed by the bold proclamation by this stranger. The old man's appearance was captivating. His black skin was almost luminescent in its smooth, deep sheen. Though he was clearly at least in his seventies, he projected an ageless quality.

Huff stepped forward. "It's that obvious?"

"Oh yes," the old man replied, "as clear as this bright blue sky that has graced us this afternoon. I sense a pain that holds the weight of many generations' sorrow."

"Man!" Huff exclaimed, putting his hands on his head and rubbing his bald scalp. "And here I was, all chill and coolin' out, thinking I was looking like all these other normal motherfuckas, and this brother sees right through me. You called me out like I was carrying a sign that says 'here comes a sad-ass dude with a miserable life.'"

The old man's brow furrowed ever so slightly and for a moment a wave of confusion crossed his face, but it passed as quickly as it had appeared. He nodded slowly and pensively.

"Indeed, my warrior friend," the old man agreed, "your lightness of step on this summer's day might lead many to assume that a lightness of heart accompanies your relaxed appearance. But as sure as the gray fog that will roll in across this lake tomorrow morning, your torment-ed spirit is only momentarily out of view."

"Warrior?" JD interjected. "You can tell he's former military?"

"As are you as well," the old man's eyes twinkled as he shifted his gaze to the shorter man. "Two brave, brave men who have shown such valor in battle." He closed his eyes and sighed. "And yet," he now stared intently into JD's eyes, "the most difficult battle is the one within."

The two veterans exchanged amazed glances again.

Something compelled JD to seize the moment. The words rolled out of his mouth before he knew it. "Can you. . .can you help my friend?" he stammered.

Again, a quizzical look from the old man. "Help your friend?"

"Yes, help my friend," JD stated, more boldly now. "You can sense his pain, you can tell it goes way back in his family, you nailed it without even knowing him."

"JD, what the hell are you..." Huff began to protest. JD cut him off.

"Sir, you seem to know so much, do you know how my friend could find peace?"

Now Huff had heard too much. "Dolan, have you lost your damn mind? Are you really puttin' my stuff out here, grasping for help from this . . ." His voice trailed off as he noticed that the old man was smiling, and nodding.

"Why yes, I can." The old man said, with an assured confidence. He gestured for both men to follow him into his stall, where he directed them to sit on a sturdy wooden bench. "I can help your friend, and I know how he can find peace."

Huff shook his head and chuckled. He took a swig from his whisky flask and looked intently at the old man. "Man oh man, this is some crazy ass shit." He looked at JD and then back at the old man. He shrugged. "Okay. Okay. What the hell? I mean, nothing else has made a damn bit of difference. Talk to me, my man, where can I find some help for my messed-up head?"

The old man stared back just as intently.

"Anomabo."

"Ano what oh?"

"Anomabo," the old man repeated.

"Anomabo. Is that a new age health clinic somewhere around here?" Huff asked.

Now it was the old man's turn to chuckle. "No, no, my warrior friend. Anomabo is my village. In the Central region. In Ghana."

"Ghana!!" Both men shouted as they leapt to their feet. "You've got to be kidding me!" Huff yelled. "JD can you believe what this. . ." his voice trailed off again as he turned to see his friend smiling broadly and nodding vigorously.

"Huff man, this is IT brother." JD stated authoritatively, eyes wide with excitement, revelation dawning on him. "This is what we have been looking for. You gotta do something radical to bust out of this funk that has you trapped. This. Is. It. Ghana!! Yes!"

Huff put both hands on top of his head and marveled at what he was hearing.

JD pressed on. "Bro, you have ALWAYS said you wanted to go to . . . what have you called it? Oh yes, the Motherland! You have always told me you wanted to go to the Motherland one day."

Huff shook his head. "Yes, for sure, but not like this! Not messed up like I am. I want to go to Africa AFTER I have gotten myself together."

"Then maybe you've had it wrong brother," JD suggested calmly. "Maybe your path to healing lies through Africa."

"It does!" The old man declared, rubbing his hands together as if the decision had been made. "Through Anomabo. The Anomabo Centre for Healing and Resilience, to be specific."

Huff and JD sat back down on the bench, clearly this was getting very serious and very real.

"You have a healing center? In Ghana? In a village in a forest somewhere?" JD asked.

"Actually, our village is on the ocean." The old man smiled. "And we built our center right on the beachfront where we and our guests can be soothed by roar of the waves and lulled by the warmth of the ocean breeze."

Huff cocked an eyebrow. "Now this is starting to sound kinda nice," he said with a grin.

JD nodded in agreement. "That sounds amazing! When can he start?"

The old man gestured at the two men. "You mean, when can you both start?" he corrected.

"Aw no man," JD responded, "we are just talking about my friend Huff here, he's the one who needs the visit to the Motherland."

The old man shook his head. "Surely you are not going to leave your friend to undertake his most profound life journey alone?"

Huff spoke up. "Sir, I'm good, I got this. I can't be dragging Dolan here clear across the world for something I gotta do."

"Ah," the old man countered, "but knowing as I do what this journey of yours will entail, I can tell you for certain that you'll be grateful for his presence after all is said and done."

Another exchange of looks between the two men, shared chuckles, and shakes of their heads. This had truly been an afternoon of surprises.

"Well," JD said, crossing his arms and smiling broadly again, "I guess this white boy is heading to the Motherland as well!" He reached out and shook the old man's hand. "So, what is your name, wise elder?"

"You can call me Baba Kofi. And I cannot wait to welcome you to Anomabo."

***

The Anomabo Centre for Healing and Resilience looked just like Huff and JD had expected based on the photos on its website. The large sign, slightly weathered and rusted, stood high and proud above the roadway leading into the complex. Symmetrical rows of palm trees stretched into the distance on either side of the road. At the end of the roadway a large cream-colored circular building stood in the center of the complex, with beautiful symbols painted on its walls. Clusters of smaller buildings were arrayed on all sides. The ocean sparkled in the distance beyond the buildings. Up and down the beach were dozens of small round cabanas with thatched roofs. Each one had a small deck facing the ocean.

Huff and JD hopped out of the SUV, stretched and yawned, both of them loosening up after the three-hour drive from the airport.

The airport arrival and the early part of their journey through the capital city of Accra had been an overwhelming cacophony of sights and sounds. Although the process of checking in through immigration and retrieving their baggage had gone relatively smoothly, the moment they stepped out of the airport terminal, their senses had been accosted by the scorching mid-afternoon heat, the aroma of grilled meat and other delicacies being served by vendors, and the sounds of joyous reunions between passengers and those picking them up. Porters and taxi drivers had swarmed around them, pulling at their arms and bags to commandeer them as customers.

They had been grateful to quickly spy the whiteboard with the words Anomabo Centre that a tall, lanky man with a broad smile was holding high above his head. He had introduced himself as Ousmane, the driver and logistics manager for the center.

They had followed him to where he parked an SUV, grateful to be able to wind their way behind someone who knew the lay of the land. They loaded their luggage in the trunk and hopped in the back seat. Ousmane handed them bottles of water which they both gulped down gratefully. He explained that he had to make a couple stops in the city to pick up supplies needed at the center and then they would get on the road for their drive to the Central region. He had thoughtfully anticipated how hungry they were and his first stop was at a street vendor where he got them each a Styrofoam container piled with fried chicken, jollof rice, bean stew, and fried plantains. They grinned at each other as they eagerly dug into their meals, knowing what they were each thinking: if this was what street vendors were serving up, they were going to be eating very well on this trip!

Ousmane's errands around the city gave them a chance to get a good sense of the sprawling capital city of Accra. They marveled at the contrasts that were immediately apparent. On the one hand, the multi-lane highways, winding overpasses, gleaming high-rise towers, and ubiquitous cranes and construction equipment conveyed the signs of a thriving, modern urban economy. Large billboards advertised the amenities of modern living: cell phones, fashion, appliances, food and alcohol, international travel. On the other hand, the array of bustling human activity that seemed to fill every possible square foot of available space gave a dizzying sense of an anything-goes free-for-all, where no one was fully in charge. A constant stream of people and animals moved in all directions and weaved among the traffic: street vendors, young and old, hawking snacks, fruit and electronics, women with goods piled on their heads and babies strapped to their backs, older men and women in traditional African clothing, young women and men in business attire, children of all ages in colorful school uniforms, stray dogs, and even cluster of goats. Both men recalled feeling this same sense of overwhelming social vibrancy on their visits to urban centers in Iraq. But Accra truly seemed like a metropolis straining at the seams of rapid urbanization.

It was a relief when Ousmane finally steered the SUV onto a highway where the traffic flowed briskly out of the city and into the countryside. The men felt their shoulders relax and breathing slow as structures thinned and wide expanses of dry savannah spread as far as their eyes could see. At several spots along the journey, the deep blue of the Atlantic Ocean could be seen stretching off into the horizon. Both men had leaned back to grab a nap.

Now, at Ousmane's direction, the two men grabbed their luggage from the trunk of the SUV and headed towards the main Anomabo building. As if on cue, Baba Kofi emerged from the front door, accompanied by a slender, older woman dressed in colorful, flowing attire and a matching head wrap. She moved gracefully towards them with a purpose of stride that matched his. He stretched his arms out wide. "Akwaaba, my American friends, welcome, welcome!" He hugged each man tightly.

He gestured to his companion, who looked even more distinguished from close-up and exuded a serene energy that had an immediate calming effect on both men. "This is my sister, Nana Afua. JD, she will be your healer for your sojourn with us."

JD shook Nana Afua's hand politely but with a confused look. "My healer?" He turned to look at Huff. "We're here for Huff's healing, yes? I'm just here to offer my guy moral support."

"Ah, dear Jonathan," Baba took both of JD's hands in his, "Yes, you are indeed here to offer your friend moral support. And, since you have come all this way, the least we can do is offer you your own restorative experience while he undergoes his." JD noticed that Nana Afua had narrowed her eyes ever-so slightly and was watching him closely with a look that made him feel like she could hear his thoughts.

"Uh, I don't know about that Baba . . .it's not exactly what I . . ." JD murmured.

"Oh, c'mon my guy!" Huff piped up, walking forward and shaking Nana's hand firmly. "Did you think you were going to sit sunning yourself while these good folks peel open my emotional layers like an onion?" He clapped JD on the back. "I thought Baba might have something up his sleeve for you as well."

JD felt a strange shiver down his spine, despite the heat and the sweat on his brow and neck. He shook it off. "You know Baba," he said, "you are absolutely right. Why come all this way and not experience all that Anomabo has to offer?"

Baba nodded appreciatively and turned and smiled at Nana, who returned his look with a gentle but determined air of resolve.

The foursome turned and walked into the circular building where the men dropped off their bags and headed off with Baba for a walking tour of the premises. He shared with them the history of the complex while indicating the sequence in which the various buildings and amenities had been constructed. They ended their tour at the beach cabanas where they would each be staying, where a staffer had already brought their bags.

"Enjoy a peaceful evening to yourselves," Baba advised. "A waiter from the restaurant will be by to take your dinner orders and will bring your meals to your cabanas. We suggest you take the evening to decompress and catch up on rest after your long travels. I would imagine you are both beer drinkers and I highly recommend you try the Club beer brewed here in Ghana – it's served in large bottles so I would suggest you only order one. We will get started bright and early tomorrow. Please give the waiter your breakfast orders as well. Breakfast will be served at 7am and we'll leave for a local tour at 8am. You two have quite a week ahead of you. Sleep well!"

***

Huff fell asleep quickly, soothed by the roar of the waves as Baba had described, and slept deeply through the night. JD also fell asleep quickly due to the travel fatigue, but, true to form, he had tossed and turned in his usual fitful restlessness and awoke several times in the night. On one of those occasions, he stirred awake drenched in sweat with his heart pounding, despite the cool ocean breeze blowing in through the windows.

"You're probably just nervous about all that is to come this week," Huff suggested, as the men ate breakfast together at Huff's cabana. "What do I have to be nervous about?" JD wondered aloud. "You're the dude riding the emotional rollercoaster with the never-ending loop."

Baba strode up to the cabana as they were finishing breakfast.

"Let me take a moment to explain our guiding principles and then give you a quick overview of what you will experience this week," he said as he sat down in the cabana. "Here at Anomabo, we understand healing to have three key precursors: safety, belonging and dignity. Only when all three are present and one does not have to trade off one for the other, can healing truly take place. We strive for safety in all its forms—physical, material, emotional, spiritual, and relational. We promote belonging as a deep sense of interconnection among people. We treat others with a sense of dignity that honors their inherent value as human beings."

He paused to let his explanation sink in.

He continued, "how often do we have to avoid connections and engagement with others, to retain a sense of safety? Or hold back from sharing our truest selves out of a fear of not being fully accepted?"

He could see that Huff and JD were reflecting on this notion of safety, belonging and dignity being in tension.

"Here at Anomabo, we emphasize safety, belonging and dignity in every facet of your experience in order to help condition you to seek harmony among the three." With this, he stood and indicated that they should follow him.

"Okay, here's how the week will proceed," Baba shared. "Today is your local orientation day. In order for you to open yourself to the healing experiences at our center, we need to briefly ground you in the historical and cultural context that surrounds Anomabo. Admittedly, one day's orientation will only barely scratch the surface of the rich history and culture of our region. But it must suffice so that we can attend to our current priority which is to help you begin to quell your inner battles. My sincere prayer for you both is that you will return to our country for an educational visit that focuses on learning more about Ghana and West Africa."

They climbed into the back of the center's van that would be their transportation for the day.

Baba went on: "After today, the rest of your time with us will settle into a familiar daily routine. We will start each day with a yoga session on the beach before breakfast. You'll then share the first communal meal of the day with staff and other guests. Then you will have a one-on-one session with your healer. We'll then give you some individual reflection time back at your cabana. We'll gather for another communal meal for lunch. You'll have rest time after lunch, during which you can opt for a massage with aromatherapy. In the afternoon, you'll have another session with your healer and then some more individual reflection time. Your evening meal is at your own discretion, you can join us for a communal meal or take your meal privately in your cabana as you did last night. We'll end each of the next few nights together down on the beach for a trauma release ritual around a fire."

He paused to see if either of the men had questions. Hearing none, he added: "And on your last day with us, we will dedicate the afternoon to a healing dance ceremony."

Huff and JD smiled excitedly at each other as they listened to what was to come. They fist bumped and suspected the other man was thinking the same thing: this week seemed well-designed to be deeply restorative. And also: how could they get out of participating in the dance ceremony?

***

Oh, how right Baba had been about the sensory and emotional whirl-wind that the men would experience throughout the course of the first day.

The morning was spent at the central market in Cape Coast, the largest town in the region, where Baba had told them they could be most quickly exposed to many dimensions of West African daily life. Both men had experienced the bustling outdoor markets of Iraq during their tours there, so they were somewhat prepared for the exceeding levels of human enterprise and economic activity in rows upon rows of market stalls. This market had certainly been as bustling and chaotic as any they had previously experienced. Every possible item that you could imagine needing to buy could be found in one of the corners of this sprawling central marketplace: fruit, vegetables, meat, fish, cloth, jewelry, luggage, household supplies, it was all here. And each purchase required a lively negotiation to arrive at a mutually agreeable price.

The morning at the market was followed by an deeply emotional experience that afternoon at the Cape Coast slave castle. When Huff had dreamed of coming to West Africa, a visit to a slave castle was one of the top priorities on his list. But he had not anticipated visiting one within twenty-four hours of setting foot on African soil. He found it jarring, a mere day after leaving the comfort of his Oakland apartment, to be suddenly walking on a group tour through dark, cramped dungeons where enslaved Africans, hundreds at a time, had been crammed together awaiting transport by ship to the west. An exchange of sober glances and dour shakes of the head between Huff and JD confirmed that they were both feeling the same way. Most devastating to both was seeing the open courtyard area where females were brought out into the daylight for the castle commander to look down from his chambers and select which one would be cleaned up and brought up for his night's pleasure.

It was the juxtapositions that were the most haunting.

The dank, gruesome dungeons below and the large, airy commander's quarters above.

The church inside the slave castle where the British occupants would worship while sitting directly above some of the greatest human brutality the world has known.

A foreboding dark tunnel in the belly of the castle led to the so-called Door of No Return through which the enslaved Africans would be marched out chained and in single file to the slaveships.

Today that tunnel opened onto a sunny beach with brightly colored fishing boats and children cavorting in the waves.

How had such horrors been perpetrated for so long? Generations upon generations of darkness and trauma. How had those massive amounts of pain and suffering been endured? Where did it live on in the bodies and minds of the victimized?

And what of the victimizers? What lasting effect had the pervasive perpetration of cruelty had on their minds, bodies, and souls?

The two men remained deep in thought for the drive back to the center from the slave castle. Huff simmered with anger and indignation at the horrors that his ancestors had endured. His personal anguish, though far less consequential than the brutality evidenced by the castle visit, seemed directly linked through generations of racial injustice. He wondered about his line of ancestry. Which slaveship had brought his ancestors to America? Might he have blood flowing in him from survivors who had passed through the very Door of No Return that he had stood in earlier?

JD was equally, if not even more, shaken by the experience. Slavery had always seemed like a distant part of history to him. Being confronted in such a tangible, immersive way with the depths of depravity on the part of his forebears unlocked a deep sense of guilt and shame within him. He could be a direct ancestor of people who had known about the slave trade and done nothing to impede it. Or, God forbid, maybe his ancestors had profited from the slave trade in some way.

His mind could not fathom all those centuries of subjugation. He thought of their stroll through the bustling marketplace that morning. He thought about the children he had watched playing at the oceanside. All of those generations of human enterprise, creativity and vitality. He felt a knot forming in his stomach at the weight of the social injustice. And how much human potential was being lost today due to enduring racial inequities and repercussions. He thought of his friend Huff and the debilitating trauma he carried. And all that he knew Huff could accomplish without that emotional burden.

Neither Huff nor JD had a restful sleep that second night. Both lay awake deeply troubled by what they had experienced. Both men felt primed for the self-examination and restoration that lay ahead. If the healing experience they had signed up for had previously seemed like an indulgence, it now felt absolutely imperative. What generational trauma were they each carrying in their own bodies?

***

Many of the daily healing activities were wonderfully soothing and physically rejuvenating—the morning beach yoga, mid-afternoon massages and aromatherapy, communal meals and light conversation with other center guests, and evenings around a beach fire. As Baba had promised, Huff could not think of a time when he had felt so safe, safe enough to completely let down his guard, had felt such a sense of belonging around people he had never met, and had felt treated with such dignity.

Huff found the trauma release beach fire activity particularly cathartic. As the guests sat around the fire each evening, center staff would hand out pieces of paper and pens. The guests would write a personal trauma or disappointment on a sheet of paper. And then one by one they would place their piece of paper into the fire. Some guests chose to verbally describe the trauma to the other guests as they burned their piece of paper, others kept this information private. Huff found himself scribing and immolating several pieces of paper each night, a welcome sense of relief flowing through his body as the smoke from each one curled up towards the night sky.

JD had a harder time thinking of something to write on the paper. Life had largely been quite smooth and happy for him. His time in the army had been the most difficult and he would always grieve the friends he had lost and all the death and destruction he had been a part of. But his re-entry to civilian had been relatively easy and he had successfully dedicated himself to his counseling sessions at the VA, and did not feel that he was carrying any lasting emotional scars from his time in battle. Eventually, reflecting back on their disturbing slave castle visit, he had written—shame for the wrongs of my ancestors—on his piece of paper and tossed it into the fire.

In contrast to these highly rejuvenating activities, their sessions with their individual healers generated moments of deep relaxation but also several intense and revealing experiences that the men found quite taxing, even haunting. It was in these individual healing sessions that the most unexpected revelations had occurred for both men.

Each of them had quickly developed a sense of trust and connection with their healer.

For Huff, this came easily since he had now experienced Baba in two very different contexts and here at Anomabo, Baba's light and positive spirit was even more infectious than in Oakland.

JD had been slower to feel connected to Nana and even over the course of several healing sessions, she remained a bit of a mystery to him. She maintained a more serious air than Baba, but she exuded a strong sense of caring and empathy, which had helped JD grow comfortable with her guidance of their time together.

***

The first healing session was on the second morning of their Anomabo visit. It started with an out-of-body, into-body exercise that both men found wonderfully centering.

In their room in the healing center, Baba guided Huff to a comfortable reclining chair and sat beside him. Nana did the same with JD in a room a few doors away.

"Relax, close your eyes and imagine floating in space, among the stars, high above the earth," the healers instructed. "Feel yourself floating weightlessly. Look around you and marvel at the brightness of the stars. Allow yourself to turn in all directions, sensing the vastness of space."

Each man felt his breathing soften as he imagined hovering in space.

The healers continued: "From where you are you can see the earth, you can make out the continents and the oceans. Now start to float down slowly and gently in the direction of the earth. Identify the western side of Africa and guide yourself towards it. As you get closer, feel yourself drawn toward the location of Ghana, and then closer still, towards our current location in Anomabo. Gently, gently, continue to descend until you can see the Anomabo complex underneath you. Allow yourself to be drawn toward the building we are currently in. As you get closer, you can see through the roof into this room. Feel a wave of familiarity and belonging ease over you as you recognize yourself sitting in this chair. Slowly descend until you are right over your body. Hover there for a few moments, appreciating this perspective on yourself, sitting there with your body relaxed and comfortable."

The healers paused to allow each man to soak in this unique vantage point on himself.

"Now let yourself glide down, slipping into your body. Feel yourself settling all the way into your body with a great ease and comfort. Now relax and savor the feeling of being wholly inside your body with your mind fully present in this moment in time and this location in space."

Both men left that morning session feeling fully embodied and present, a sensation that lingered with them throughout the rest of that day.

For the afternoon session, the healers shifted to instructing the men in relaxation and mindfulness techniques using soothing sounds and motions.

The healers directed them to begin by humming slowly and steadily. Immediately the inner vibrations pulsing throughout their body generated a sense of calm. At first, the healers had them simply sustain a slow, steady hummmmmm. Then they were encouraged to experiment with higher and lower pitches to see which ones felt most soothing. Then they were asked to select a familiar tune and hum it all the way through.

Next the men were instructed to create a buzzing sound by placing their tongue behind their two front teeth and vibrating it rapidly.

Then they shifted from buzzing to making a deep ohm sound. And they held the ohmmmmmm longer and longer.

Next the healers had them add a gentle rocking motion while making the sounds.

They closed out the afternoon session combining the sounds and motions which they had found most soothing.

They spent the second morning session practicing the sound and motion techniques they had learned the day before.

In the afternoon session, the healers shifted their focus to grounded breathing.

Huff's afternoon session went quite smoothly. "Ok Richard," Baba instructed him, "keep your eyes open but relax into a soft gaze. Open your senses to the environment around you. Sense the soft light emanating around the room. Listen for the sounds that you can hear near and far. Sniff the air and see what scents you can pick up. Now take several slow, deep breaths, in through the nose and out through your mouth."

Huff complied and felt the tension leaving his body and his heart rate slowing.

Baba continued: "Now focus on your body. Feel the weight of your body pressing down into the chair. Allow each body part touching the chair to completely relax into the surface. Feel the soles of your feet on the ground. Sense the solid base that the ground provides for your feet and for the rest of your body. Now focus on your breath and its path within your body. As you exhale, trace the sensation of the breath flowing out from your core into your extremities."

Baba nodding approvingly as Huff breathed deeply and slowly.

"Now Richard, I want you to think of a person who brings safety and stability in your life. When you are in their presence, you feel a deep sense of comfort." Huff envisioned JD and smiled instinctively. "Now scan your body from head to toe and check in with each of your body parts in this relaxed state." Baba gave Huff several moments to complete this process.

"Ok now, imagine that the comforting person is gone and in their place is now an angry stranger. You can sense their negative emotions directed at you. Scan yourself from head to toe once again. This time, pay particular attention to the areas of your body where you feel constriction and tightness." Huff marveled at how quickly tension had formed in his forehead, his neck, his shoulders, and his lower back. Baba's soothing voice interjected, "Okay, now send the angry stranger away. Bring the comforting person back and revel in their soothing presence. Scan your body one more time and this time linger on the areas that are softest and most relaxed."

After this exercise, Huff felt extremely rejuvenated.

A few doors over, JD had a very different experience. He settled comfortably into the reclining chair and Nana walked him through the sound and motion activities and then the process of sensing the external environment and then the process of turning his attention inwards. She helped him slow his breathing and let the tension ease from his muscles. Upon being invited to envision a comforting person, JD imagined his mother holding him in a loving hug.

"Okay John, that's very good," Nana said gently. "Now imagine that the comforting person is replaced by an angry stranger." JD immediately felt his face tighten into a frown and his stomach muscles contract. He willed himself to try to stay relaxed but instead he felt his heart rate quicken. Nana instructed him: "Now John, do another scan from head to toe, identifying everywhere you feel tension."

JD could hear her voice but was fixated on the image of the angry stranger which was stalking closer and closer to him. Nana's voice seemed to grow faint as the stranger's face grew closer and his features became more prominent. JD could now make out an angular face, pale skin, cold, cruel eyes and a scraggly goatee. His breath grew shallower, and he now felt tightness in his chest.

"Okay John," Nana guided, "now send the angry stranger away and invite the comforting person back." JD could faintly hear her instructions and attempted to comply, but the stranger shook his head and seemed to be refusing to leave. JD's frown intensified. Go away, go away, he repeated in his mind. The stranger's visage seemed to hover in place in front of him and JD could see the side of his mouth turn up into a sneer. JD's forehead wrinkled in consternation.

Sensing his distress, Nana took his face in her warm hands and gently called to him. "John, hear my voice. Breath in deeply and when you exhale, blow the stranger far away from you." JD took in a deep breath as instructed and then let out a huge release of air. The stranger's face seemed to evaporate. JD's shoulders relaxed and he took a few more deep breaths.

"You can gently open your eyes," Nana said.

JD opened his eyes slowly and let out one more big breath. "Woah, that was intense!" he exclaimed. "Is that normal for that exercise?"

Nana nodded slowly. "Everyone's experiences can be very different. You certainly had a very strong reaction to the angry stranger." She narrowed her eyes. "Clearly your experiences in Ghana so far, combined with your early healing activity, have surfaced something powerful and important. Don't worry, it would not have happened if you were not ready to work through it." She encouraged JD to focus on relaxing the rest of that evening and not to worry too much about what he had experienced.

The morning session of the third day was dedicated, once again, to practicing their new mindfulness and relaxation techniques.

After Huff had settled into the reclining chair for the afternoon session on the third day, Baba informed him: "we will be exploring family trauma this afternoon." Huff felt his stomach tighten and Baba could sense his tension. "I can imagine you'd prefer to avoid this my friend, but this is where we need to delve in and do some real work together." Huff had nodded soberly, leaned back and closed his eyes.

Baba led Huff through some grounding breathing exercises and then started with a first question. "Let's start with your mother. What life events may have caused most trauma for her?"

A litany of harms came to mind as soon as Huff reflected on his mother's difficult life journey. He shared with Baba his mom's travails of a difficult childhood growing up in poverty, the abandonment by his father, and her turning to drugs as a coping mechanism which had brought her into contact with people and places that only brought more trauma into her life.

"How about your father?" Baba asked.

Again, Huff had no problem generating numerous instances of suffering that his father had endured. Though he had named them before to himself and to others, many times, for some reason sharing them now felt like more of a release, in the context of everything else he had experienced so far that week.

Baba commended him. "That's very good Richard, thank you for sharing all of that. Now, tell me, how did those traumatic events affect the choices that they each made in life?"

"Aw man Baba. In so many ways," Huff replied. "In fact, I can't think of any choices they made, particularly all their bad choices, that were NOT influenced by the trauma they have experienced."

"I understand," Baba said gently, "and so how did that trauma affect how they raised you?"

Now tears began to stream down Huff's face.

"Take your time," Baba said, as he laid a comforting hand on Huff's shoulder.

"It affected . . ." Huff began to speak, but his sobs became stronger and he could not talk for several moments. His broad shoulders convulsed as he let the tears flow.

"Use your breathing," Baba encouraged him. "Breath deeply my friend, ground yourself here and now. Use your humming. Use your calming motions."

Huff began to hum softly, wrapped his arms around himself, and began to sway gently as he hummed.

"Man that feels good," he said a few moments later as he opened his eyes.

"Now tell me," Baba prodded.

Huff took one more deep breath and exhaled slowly. "The trauma they experienced affected everything about how they raised me. Every single thing. They were just playing out the worst of everything they had experienced. The pain. The fear. The rejection."

"And now, how about your grandparents?" Baba asked.

"Woah, we're going back there, huh?" Huff responded.

"Oh, yes, we've got to trace this back," Baba affirmed. "What traumatic events did your grandparents experience?"

"Honestly, man, I really can't say too much about them. My parents both left home as teenagers and did not stay close to their parents. I actually never met any of my grandparents."

"Ah Richard," Baba said thoughtfully, "now that in itself is a form of trauma, the sense of disconnection you have lived with not experiencing directly your ancestry prior to your parents."

"I never thought about it that way," Huff admitted. "And, come to think of it, there is one piece of family history that my father told me one time, but it was so painful and so distant, and I was so young, I just forgot about it." He shivered now and wrinkled his forehead as the memory came back to him.

"And what was that piece of family history, Richard?"

"My father once told me that his grandfather had been lynched. In Starkville, Mississippi. In broad daylight. It was at a July 4th celebration. The town was gathering anyway, so they held the lynching that day." Huff clenched his jaw and his veins protruded on his temples. "Can you imagine? All those men, women and children gathered to celebrate the holiday, eating their hot dogs and apple pie, and watching my great-grandfather strung up to his death." He took a deep breath and then another one. "Apparently he was trying to start a banking business, to offer blacks an alternative way to manage their money. He was warned by the local white leaders not to proceed with his plan, but he went ahead anyway."

"I am so sorry Richard," Baba sighed. "Do you know what happened to your great-grandmother after that?"

"Yes," Huff replied, "she got my grandfather and his siblings out of town as soon as possible. That's what led to that side of the family moving north to Chicago."

"Thank you for releasing that," Baba stated solemnly. He took both of Huff hands in his and both men sat in silence for a few minutes. And then Baba led Huff in some more breathing exercises to close out the session.

Down the hall, JD had a far less intense session on family trauma.

Nana had guided him through some breathing activities to get settled and centered. And then she had posed the same question as

Baba: "What life events may have caused the most trauma for your mother?"

JD thought for a few moments. "I gotta say I can't really think of much," he said. "She and my dad always seemed pretty rock solid and they each had a pretty smooth path through life. I guess the most traumatic had to be the miscarriage she had when they were first trying to start a family. She never talked about it, but I know from my dad that it was the most difficult time of their marriage. She wanted a family so badly, they both did, and that must have really rocked their world and created an uncertainty that they may not have ever felt before. But I think it was not too long after that that she got pregnant with me, and...as you can see, that worked out pretty well for me and for them!"

Nana smiled. "How did that affect choices your parents made? And how did it affect how they raised you?"

"That's a great question," JD replied, cocking his head to the side as he considered Nana's query. "Now that I think about it, it kinda explains a whole lot."

"Like what?"

"Well, like how cherished and treasured I felt as a child. My parents always made me feel like I was a special gift to them. And my siblings as well, we never felt like we were any kind of burden to them. In fact, my mom used to hold me close and say 'thank you for being here with us.' Which I always found strange as a boy because, I mean, where else would I be? Did I have any choice??"

Nana waited for JD to continue.

"And we had a less adventurous life than most folks. Stayed in the same town for decades, my folks stayed in the same jobs. As I got older it became clear to me that my folks did not like uncertainty and seemed to always play it pretty safe." He chuckled, "My decision to enlist after

9-11 really freaked them out." The smile left his face. "As I think about it now, my time in Iraq was probably the second most traumatic thing that had ever happened to them. I was just focused on serving our country after what had happened to us, I never really thought about the impact on them." He paused reflectively. "But it all worked out! And I know they are as proud as hell of me."

"And what about your grandparents?" Nana asked. "Any traumatic events in their lives?"

"Hmmm, not that I know of," JD responded. "It's likely that they would not have shared much, they were the focus-on-the-positive types, not ones to dwell on the dark side of things."

Suddenly he sat up in his chair.

"You know, that makes me realize..."

"Realize what, John?"

"I realize that there was something about our family history that they avoided talking about. I think it goes way back, like to the time of my grandmother's parents. I just always got the sense that there was something back there that they were ashamed of. My siblings and I used to talk among ourselves about it when we were young and my mom's parents were still living. There was something about the ways things would get quiet and folks would look uncomfortable when certain topics would come up."

Nana's eyes narrowed in the way that had become very familiar to JD. "Like what kinds of topics?"

"I dunno," John lay back and reclined once more. "Topics about the past. Like about their lives down south where they grew up."

"Really. That's very interesting John," Nana mused. "Do you know where your great-grandparents grew up in the south?"

"Starkville, Mississippi."

***

After the usual routine of breathing and humming exercises on the morning of their fourth day, the healers informed each man that they would be working on a Tree of Life exercise that day to do some mapping of their personal and family history, some more pruning of hurts and regrets, and some visioning about the future.

The healers presented each man with a worksheet on a clipboard. The top sheet was a diagram of a tree. The second sheet was a set of instructions. The healers gave each man a chance to read over the instructions.

Tree of Life

INSTRUCTIONS

You will use this Tree of Life worksheet exercise to map your past, present and future. Your Tree of Life includes four key elements: the Roots, the Trunk, the Branches, and the Leaves. There are also nourishing elements, the rays of sunshine, that will help your Tree flourish. There are also destructive elements, harmful insects, that will damage your tree.

The Roots

Around the roots of the tree write where you come from and where your parents, relatives and ancestors come from. What town or village do you come from? What town or village do your parents come from? What town or village do your grandparents come from? Roots also include the people, places and organizations that have supported and cared for you in your life.

The Trunk

The trunk of the tree contains your formative experiences, good and bad. On the right side of the tree write down some of the good events in your life. What made you happy? What are the times you celebrated? On the left side of the tree, write about some of the difficult times in your life.

The Branches

The branches of the tree are your aspirations for your life. On the branches, write some of your biggest hopes and goals for the future.

The Leaves

The leaves are your abilities that will help you achieve your goals. On the leaves, write the characteristics, talents and skills that will help you to achieve those future aspirations.

The Sunshine

On the rays of sunshine, write the positive factors in your life that will support your process of achieving your aspirations.

Harmful Insects

Finally, name some of the harmful insects that are the obstacles in your life, internal and external, that make it harder for you to achieve your hopes.

Both men appreciated the change of pace from the previous days of intense one-on-one practice and delved into the exercise with enthusiasm. They spent the remainder of the morning session filling out the worksheet, and then the healers instructed them to finish completing it on their own before the afternoon session.

Returning for his afternoon session, Huff proudly handed his completed worksheet to Baba. Baba took a few minutes to read through it, stroking his beard thoughtfully.

"Ok Richard, very good," he said eventually. "Thank you for taking this exercise so seriously."

He led Huff through some centering exercises.

"Ok, now to your Tree of Life," Baba stated. "What was most striking to you as you filled this out?"

"A few things," Huff replied. "Tracing my roots and where we are all from got me thinking more deeply about my family than I have in a long, long time. In fact, I've really come to think of them as a non-factor in my life because I've had to be so self-sufficient. But the fact is, so much of me is them. So much of my path was influenced by their paths." He shook his head slowly. "And then I had to decide where to put my family as I filled out the trunk of the tree. It was easy to quickly put them on the bad, challenging side, and certainly they belong there. But I then realized there was much about them that belonged on the positive side as well."

"Such as?" Baba prodded.

"Well, such as my parent's resilience and fortitude. For so long I've been thinking of everything I've had to do to survive and push forward, and I haven't thought much about what they had to endure and overcome. I also put my mom's sense of humor on the positive side of the trunk. Despite all she was going through, she always had the ability to find a funny angle to any predicament. I realized this is one of my leaves on my tree – my sense of humor."

"Anything else?" Baba asked.

"Yeah. Something big. The branches of the tree really got me think-ing. It's been a long time since I allowed myself to dream big. To set big goals. I've just kinda been going through the motions. I haven't wanted to put any hopes on my future until I could feel better about my present. Walking through that marketplace in Cape Coast and seeing all that entrepreneurial activity. Stall after stall after where an enterprising person had to decide to take a risk – they had taken whatever they had access to, and turned it into a business. It sparked my own sense of enterprise. I thought of seeing your stall at the Lake Merritt festival, Baba. You seemed so proud to be able to make those artifacts available to customers so far across the ocean from your home."

Baba smiled. "Yes, it is indeed a joy."

"So I've committed to starting my own side business. I'm very handy and I like fixing things. I've always done all my own repairs at home. At my delivery job, they've been asking me to help with minor repairs in the office building. I have a buddy with a handyman business that is doing very well and I'm going to ask him to help me get my own business started."

"That is wonderful Richard," Baba said encouragingly. "And I can see you've listed many leaves and rays of sunshine that can help you achieve that goal. So, let's focus on these harmful insects, shall we? The two that stand out to me are fear and self-doubt."

Huff nodded.

"What are you afraid of Richard?"

Huff mulled the question over. Baba was pleased to see him applying his breathing techniques, inhaling and exhaling slowly and evenly. Not feeling rushed to compose an answer.

"Certainly fear of failure. I guess that's the big one. What if I try this and can't pull it off. I mean, no one in my family ever owned a business. And I've never done anything like this."

"Totally understandable," Baba responded. "But think of it this way, my warrior friend. If you never try this, you will have failed to act upon an aspiration that you have. That will be a failure for sure.

So you can accept that certain failure, or you can give it a try and give yourself a chance at success."

"I never really saw it that way," Huff mused.

"And this self-doubt you mention," Baba continued. "It is clear from all that you have written on the trunk of your tree that the shortcomings of your family and all the adversity in your life has given you good reason to question your self-worth and your abilities. But I also see so much that you have listed here that suggests a life of value and potential – your loyalty and dependability, your ability to not take yourself or anything too seriously, your ability to connect with people from all different types of backgrounds and to quickly engender their trust."

Huff nodded.

"But perhaps most important is that you've named this obstacle for yourself. You've admitted your doubts, which I'm sure is not easy for a fighter like yourself."

Huff snorted. "You sure got that right." He took the Tree of Life diagram from Baba. He traced the outline of the tree with his finger, from the roots, along the trunk, and out to the branches.

"Thank you Baba," he said, as he tapped the diagram.

***

A few doors down, JD was also marveling at some revelations that his Tree of Life exercise had generated for him.

"So John, what did you find most striking, as you filled out the worksheet?" Nana had asked.

"Number one, my handwriting really sucks."

"I have to agree with you there," Nana chuckled, "I'm going to need you to decipher some of these scratchings for me."

"Well," JD grew more serious, "the exercise confirmed what I've always known but perhaps haven't appreciated as much as I should have. Man, I've had a lot going for me every step of the way. Good solid roots, a healthy trunk, a lot of leaves and sunshine. I'm one lucky son of a bitch."

"You are indeed John, your tree seems to be flourishing."

"But here's the thing," John continued, "until this week, until this time with you all here, I've felt pretty comfortable just flourishing by myself, with my friends."

Having reviewed his diagram, Nana knew what was coming.

"Watching those children playing at the beach at Cape Coast Castle, really got me. Their playfulness, their innocence, all the life that lies ahead of them. Nana, I'm suddenly feeling ready to be a dad and bring some bambinos into this world." His smile was as big as she'd seen it.

"But the wild thing that has really got my mind spinning and my heart pumping is that it's not just about the playful times. Seeing those children playing in *this* place, with *this* history, and all this unfinished, unresolved need to repair the evils of the past. I'm suddenly seeing my role in it. Not just as an individual, but as an ancestor myself. You all, this place, the reflections, this Tree of Life, you've got me thinking about a long line of Dolans passing along good stuff and passing along bad stuff." He thumped his chest. "I'm ready to start passing along some good stuff!"

He shook his head. "I've rarely thought about my own ancestors, let alone thought of myself as an ancestor. Nor have I thought about all that we hold in our minds and in our bodies that we literally pass down from generation to generation. For better and for worse."

He looked intently at Nana.

"Being here with Huff. Seeing how he is unlocking and releasing things he has held inside. Having the chance to focus on myself and seeing the questions I have failed to ask myself. Being confronted with the suffering and inequity in this world. And all the shame about it that I now realize that I carry in my body."

He smiled. "I'm ready to be a healthier presence in this world."

***

The healing session the next morning was again dedicated to extended time practicing various breathing techniques. Given the weightiness of the conversations and revelations the day before, both men were grateful for the light and easy session.

As they settled into their reclining chairs that afternoon, the healers informed them that for their final session, they would once again be delving back into their personal lineage. This time they would be inviting the presence of an ancestor and seeking to make a connection that might yield useful learning and insights.

Huff reclined comfortably and centered himself with some slow breathing.

"Clear your mind as best you can," Baba instructed. "Envision the starry sky. Remember the expanse of space as you floated in it. Feel the openness around you. Open your mind, open your heart, open your spirit to all that is around you."

Huff felt all the muscles in his body relax and let his thoughts drift away and the image of the expansiveness of space filled his consciousness.

"Good Richard," Baba encouraged. "Now, from deep in your heart, from the most meaningful place you can imagine inside, invite an ancestor to join you. Let them know your heart is willing and ready to receive their energy."

Huff imagined a warm energy flowing from inside him and emanating outwards. As it passed through his body he layered an invitation into it: come to me ancestor, I am truly open to your presence.

Almost immediately he felt another energy sensation pushing against the energy flowing from his body. The energy was warm and light and he relaxed and let the energy flow into him. He heard Baba's voice, though it sounded far away.

"Stay relaxed Richard. Let your ancestor's presence seek its own course."

Huff resisted the urge to query the energy or influence it in any way. He breathed as slowly as he could and remained as calm and still as possible.

Then, at first barely perceptibly and then more clearly, a. . .how to describe it . . .sense of *meaning* began to emerge from the energy. Not quite a sound. Not quite words or language. More a feeling than anything he could actually envision.

He breathed slowly and patiently, focusing on keeping his heart and mind open and relaxed.

He began to have the keen sense of a female presence. A mother? No, older. A grandmother? No, even more aged, more timeless, more . . .ancestral? Ah, a great-grandmother. Yes, somehow he knew he was in the presence of his great-grandmother. And her energy was so. . .so, what? So defiant. So determined. Oh the strength that was pulsing in that energy now. And the—meaning—was becoming even more perceptible.

We. Have. Survived.

The meaning felt so pure and so true.

We. Have. Survived.

And then, the energy grew even warmer and more radiant.

You. Have. Survived.

You. Must. Survive.

You. Will. Survive.

The energy began to fade. And then pulsed once more.

We. Will. Survive.

Tears were coursing down his face now, though his body remained still and his breathing remained steady.

Baba, sensing the ancestor's visit had ended, laid his hands on Huff's shoulders.

"Be at peace, dear warrior, be at peace."

***

In his healing session, JD was in for a far more disruptive experience.

Nana helped him relax, and open his mind and heart. His breathing slowed and he relaxed as much as he could.

"Okay John, now invite an ancestor to join you. Send them a message of welcome."

Like Huff, JD had sensed a warm energy emanating from within him and radiating outwards. He smiled at the new sensation, proud of his newfound relationship with his body and its energy flow.

His self-congratulatory vibe was interrupted by the emerging sense of another energy presence. At first, it was just a faint sense of an energy vibrating differently from the energy emanating from him. But as it became stronger, it felt . . .ominous. Somehow it felt discordant, troubled, out of sync. The memory of his previous disconcerting experience with the visit from a stranger exercise now rushed back to him and his breathing quickened and his muscles tensed.

Nana sensed his distress. "Easy John, easy," she instructed. "Keep breathing. Hum if you need to. Stay open. Keep your heart open."

JD formed an ohm sound deep in his abdomen and exhaled as slowly as he could.

The discordant energy continued to grow in magnitude, but something about it felt . . what? Scared? Remorseful? Ashamed?

JD feelings of fear subsided and were replaced by a sense of empathy. He could recognize the hollow energy of shame in the ancestor's presence.

He exhaled again and tried to exude comforting energy.

The discordant energy now began to sharpen. He shuddered as he felt he could make out a shrill-pitched vibration reminiscent of screams. And he could now sense distinct colors. How strange. Red, white and . . .blue? Yes, red, white and blue. The red and white coalesced into alternating stripes, as the blue settled into a solid shape of its own. And then...stars? Yes, white stars formed within the blue.

And then, horrifically, he could make out the dark form of a body. Hanging. Swinging.

He sat transfixed.

It was one more stark juxtaposition. The familiar Stars and Stripes, about which he was so proud and for which he was willing to give his own life. And the unmistakable shrieks of anguish and grief as a dark body swayed back and forth.

And then, one more feeling emerged alongside the shame and remorse. . . responsibility.

An understanding formed in his mind.

We. Did. This.

He tensed. The weightlessness with which he had started the exercise had long been replaced by a feeling of heaviness.

He allowed the sense of responsibility to settle deep upon and within him. He breathed steadily. And then, with an intentionality and sense of control which he could not have summoned just days earlier, he released the responsibility back out of his body and into the space around him with a long, slow, purposeful exhale.

Nana placed her hands gently on his shoulders.

JD opened his eyes and looked at her with determination.

"We did this," he stated. "And we can heal this."

He nodded to himself.

"Starting with me."

***

JD walked over to Huff's cabana, where they had agreed to have their dinner together, away from the group, to reflect on their afternoon healing sessions.

Huff was gazing off into the horizon. His look had a combination of wonder and appreciation that JD could not ever remember seeing.

"Looks like you had quite a final session," JD said as he placed his hand on his friend's shoulder.

Huff shook his head reflectively. "Brother, you have NO idea."

"Oh, I think I do, my man," JD countered, "Here I was thinking that this trip was all about you and your healing, and I ended up going on a deep dive of my own. And this afternoon went to a whole other level."

Huff turned to look at JD, a grin widening on his face. "That's so great JD. This was all about me, and you were here for me. But who knew you would have gotten something so meaningful for yourself?"

JD nodded. "Yeah, crazy."

He rubbed his fingers through his beard while shaking his head.

"And to think it all led back to Starkville."

Huff almost jumped out of his chair.

"What did you say!?" he exclaimed, causing JD to flinch at the sudden outburst.

"It all led back to Starkville," JD explained, "it's a small town in Mississippi."

"I know where Starkville is!" Huff fairly growled, "What the hell do YOU know about Starkville?"

"It's where my people on my mom's side are from," JD said slowly, getting a prickly sensation throughout his body as he realized another revelation was unfolding between them. "I've never met anyone who had heard of it. What's your connection?"

"Bro, it's where MY people are from, on my dad's side."

"No shit!?"

"No shit, dude."

"Damn."

They let this crazy, cosmic coincidence settle over them.

Neither man spoke for several moments.

"They had to get the fuck out of there though," Huff finally stated.

JD's skin tingled. His chin dropped to his chest and his eyes fell to his feet.

"The lynching," he said softly.

"WHAT!?!?!" Huff leapt to his feet, glaring at JD intensely. "What did you say?"

"I said it was the lynching." He looked up at Huff with a look that was both haunted and knowing. "Now I get it. Now I get . . .us."

Huff struggled to get the words out. "How the hell do you know about the lynching?" he sputtered.

JD stood and put his arms gently on both of Huff's shoulders. He took a deep breath.

"Because my people were there."

He continued, "fuck Huff, my people may have been part of it for all I know. But I do know they were there."

Huff pulled away and sat down heavily.

"Woah." He stared ahead blankly now.

"Woah," he repeated. "It was July 4th," he said, shaking his head.

"July 4th." JD echoed. "That's why I saw the flag. My God. Even on our national holiday."

Huff looked quizzically at JD, but did not bother to ask.

Tears were streaming down JD's face now.

"Huff. I am so, so deeply sorry. For . . .everything. For every damn thing."

"I know you are, my man," Huff replied, his own face wet with tears as well. He stood and grabbed JD into the firmest and longest embrace the two men had ever shared. "I know you are."

***

For the final morning of their stay, the healers gave the men individual time to reflect and journal on their experiences and insights. Both men were grateful for the time alone to sit with the weight of what had been revealed the day before.

That afternoon, they gathered with the staff, other guests, and a troupe of dancers and musicians from the village for the healing dance ceremony. As they sat watching the preparations for the ceremony, JD leaned over to Huff and whispered, "Do you think there's any way we can get out of this, man?" Huff had whispered back, "Not a chance, I already asked Baba. He said it's a vital part of the healing process." JD shook his head. "I don't see how embarrassment and humiliation is a useful step, especially after all that we've both been through."

But as the drums began to pound out a driving rhythm and the dancers began to stomp and whirl, both men found themselves nodding along and tapping their feet. By the time two of the dancers came over to them and invited both men out into the circle, they were good and ready to join the joyful throng. Huff leapt into the fray confidently and moved vigorously and rhythmically to the beat, raising his knees high and twirling his arms as he saw the dancers doing. JD started out more cautiously, at first jumping in place to the rhythm and bouncing his head from side to side. Then, gaining in confidence and unleashing a carefree spirit, he began waving his arms over his head and kicking his legs in front and behind him.

The two men danced, and danced, and danced, casting off the woes of generations past.

***

"Only one place to close out our last night in Ghana," JD stated with a smile, strolling up to Huff holding two Club beers. He handed one to his best friend. The musicians and the dancers had dispersed and the guests were clustered in groups as their last evening at the center wound down.

"I know that's right," Huff agreed, a broad grin on his face as well, "I hear the waves calling us."

The two men strolled down to the oceanfront and settled into two reclining beach chairs.

They sat silently, sipping their beers. A serene energy flowed between and around them. The rhythmic roar of the waves was reminiscent of the pounding drum beat of the healing dance ceremony. The vast black sky was teeming with brightly sparkling stars. It was not hard to imagine that each star was an ancestor, twinkling with delight for the healing that had been achieved that week. Twinkling for the intergenerational trauma that would be passed down no further.

Eventually as their breathing slowed, their eyes began to droop, and their heads nodded with drowsiness, they roused themselves, gave each other a firm, extended hug, then headed for their beach cabanas.

John Dolan slept through the night for the first time in his adult life.

Author's Reflection

This story was deeply influenced by the work of Resmaa Menakem, the psychotherapist who has pioneered somatic abolitionism, the practice of recognizing and processing the trauma of "White body supremacy" that resides in all our bodies. His groundbreaking work is *My Grandmother's Hands: Racialized Trauma and the Pathway to Mending Our Hearts and Bodies*.

Originally my aim was to focus the story on a Black protagonist who goes through an arc of healing his embodied intergenerational trauma. With a closer study of Menakem's work, I was blown away by the revelation that White people hold their own intergenerational racialized trauma in their bodies as well, and that in fact the path to eliminating racism in society requires that White people face up to their own trauma, not just that which they have inflicted upon Black people. With this epiphany, the story was vastly deepened to the tale of two friends with a head fake towards the Black friend as protagonist but the White friend being the one whose healing from trauma is actually the center of the story. Readers will note that the story begins and ends with John Dolan, not Richard Huffman.

Many of the somatic healing exercises in the story are drawn directly, or modified, from exercises Menakem provides in *My Grandmother's Hands*. Other exercises, such as the Tree of Life, are modified from other healing practices I found as I prepared for the story.

I always knew that the healing journey for the characters would include a visit to West Africa, where I have spent a number of years, both as a child and as an adult. On trips to Ghana over the past decade and a half with my father, with my wife and kids, and leading a study abroad experience for graduate students, the time I've spent soothed by the ocean winds and waves has been particularly rejuvenating for me. While The Anomabo Centre for Healing and Resilience is a fictional place, there is an Anomabo Beach Resort located just a short drive from the Cape Coast Slave Castle which, as many readers will already know, is also a very real, devastatingly real, place.

More on the principles of healing espoused at the Anomabo Centre—and the role of safety, dignity and belonging—can be found in the work of Prentis Hemphill, her book is *What It Takes To Heal: How Transforming Ourselves Can Change The World*, and Staci Haines, as described in her book *The Politics of Trauma: Somatics, Healing and Social Justice*.

How has this story expanded your understanding of intergenerational trauma and the ways in which it resides in our bodies?

What intergenerational trauma might you be carrying, and how can you avoid passing it to future generations?

Which healing practices might you add to your own wellness routine and antiracism journey?

Divine Restitution

The Divinity

Humans could be so much better than this.

I am perplexed and deeply disappointed by the failure of my latest effort to nudge humanity toward the more equitable future I have always intended for them. For eons I have kept watch over the creation I set in motion, patiently waiting for my aspiration for this species to be fulfilled. Love is the most powerful force in the universe and I have endowed humankind with a capacity for love never before brought into existence.

And yet.

And yet, despite my small and big nudges throughout history, humankind continues to follow progress with retrenchment, liberation with domination, enlightenment with ignorance.

What humans called the COVID-19 pandemic was my latest nudge.

And for a moment I thought it might be the breakthrough I have yearned for.

Such marvels were achieved, so quickly. Oh, how far humans have come in their scientific, economic and operational prowess!

They financed, invented, and disseminated vaccines with remarkable speed and efficiency. In government and philanthropy humans moved quickly to circumvent decades of bureaucracy to accelerate access to care.

And yet.

And yet I had aimed for so much more.

COVID-19, like the acceleration of climate change set in motion years before it, was a phenomenon that literally affected every single human being on earth. It had pained me to enable these conditions to unfurl with such ferocity against the human race.

But just as with the ancient flood that I had used as a reset for civilization in the time of Noah, I aimed to give humans yet another chance to transcend their greed, fear, and xenophobia. With the shared vulnerability created by these extreme dangers, I had hoped that human beings, and the nations, corporations, and alliances they had formed to organize themselves, would finally see how much their commonality outweighed their differences. That they would finally be prompted to make right the inequities spawned by generations of exploitation of those seen as the other, particularly those of darker complexions.

It was not to be.

While the reach of COVID-19 was universal, its impacts were not equitable. Populations marginalized by race and class were far more vulnerable to these effects and were left to suffer much more from the lethality of the virus. Advanced nations hoarded the vaccines for themselves, only sharing broadly once they had excess.

And once again I witnessed the perverse irony that some companies and industries found a way to benefit from this worldwide calamity through the callous wonders of capitalism, the human invention designed to enable the few to benefit from the distress and deprivation of the many.

The very same has been true of the recent accelerating impacts of climate change. A chance for unified global action and solidarity, largely squandered by humankind.

And so, this time I will try something very different.

***

60 Minutes Investigative Report
A Very Different Pandemic

Good evening viewers, our next news story is still unfolding across the country and indeed the world, but we now know enough to share with you the initial results of some investigative reporting on what appears to a very different pandemic.

As most of you know by now, it first seemed that we were experiencing a replay of COVID-19.

A mysterious virus began to afflict an increasing number of individuals, spreading with stunning speed across populations and geographies. This virus was even more contagious than COVID-19. It seemed to linger in the air longer, survive on surfaces more tenaciously, was impervious to conventional hand sanitizers, and was able to penetrate even N95 masks.

The World Health Organization and world governments sprang into emergency action, halting travel and implementing lockdowns with which the people across the world anxiously but dutifully complied. The sophisticated vaccine production industry cranked into gear to deploy its capabilities against the new foe.

And then, just as quickly as the world leapt into crisis mode, the red alert was lifted.

Though fiendishly contagious, it turns out that the virus has blessedly limited effects, even more mild than the common cold. It causes a 72-hour period of itchy eyes and frequent sneezing among the afflicted, and then vanishes without a trace, leaving the individual no worse for wear. There are no lasting effects.

Among most people.

It took a few weeks for the astonishing realities of the new virus to become widely apparent.

For the details of this stunning discovery, let's go to my conversation with Dr. Sally Robinson, Director of the Infectious Diseases Pathology Branch of the Centers for Disease Control and Prevention in Atlanta.

Dr. Robinson, how did the strange effects of the new virus first come to light?

"The spontaneous healings were the first sign."

Spontaneous healings?

"Yes, news outlets across the U.S. began reporting stories of mysterious healing events in which people who had been severely injured in accidents—car crashes, building fires, workplace mishaps—had been miraculously and fully healed on the spot by bystanders who had come to their aid."

Healed by bystanders?

"That's right. Eyewitnesses reported how, at the mere touch of the bystander, the injured person ceased their anguish, became fully calm, and in the full view of those around, their bodies repaired themselves.

The person stood up, able to walk away under their own power. Video documentation of these healings went viral on social media."

And that's not the only astonishing thing about these healings, right?

"Absolutely right. Another remarkable aspect of these healings has quickly become clear. The identity of the healing bystander in each of these situations. A common thread to every single occurrence."

Yes, go on.

"In each of these mysterious healings, the bystander was a Black woman."

A Black woman.

So Black women are doing all this healing?

"Yes, it appears so. African-American women who have been infected with the virus have suddenly developed an ability to heal injuries through touch. We don't yet understand the medical science behind this, but after hundreds of instances, we can confirm that this healing power is very real."

And that is not the only new power these women have gained, correct?

"Well, yes, this is where things get even more . . .ummm, hard to explain."

Please tell us more.

"Okay, well we now know that there are at least two other powers that these women have developed."

Two additional powers?

"Yes, one is the power to ease anxiety and fear. There is now ample evidence that simply with their physical presence, these women can calm the energy in the room around them."

Fascinating. Please tell us more about the evidence for this.

"Well, there are numerous reports and videos of loud, raucous environments, it could be a school board meeting, a neighborhood street basketball game, an automakers union meeting, even gang fights and political protests, that have been instantly transformed into a tranquil setting the moment an African-American woman entered the space."

And this calming effect works through physical presence?

"Yes, just as the healing power requires proximity and touch, so too this calming effect only worked for those in the near vicinity of the women. And what's most interesting that there are usually still strong disagreements taking place, but in the presence of Black women, calm and courteous deliberations prevail."

And there's a third power?

"Yes, this one is perhaps the most hard to believe. The Black women infected by the virus now have the ability to discern a lie from the truth."

My goodness. The power of truth-telling.

"That's right. Apparently, immediately upon hearing the utterance of a falsehood, these women have an instinctive sense that the statement is untrue. Not only that, they are also able to call to mind the actual truth. When they so choose, they can reveal the falsehood and correct the facts."

I imagine this particular power was slower to come to light.

"Precisely. We are learning that at first, these women kept this power to themselves, not being clear on what was happening. Then they began to confront their spouses and family members about misleading statements. Then they began to call out their friends and co-workers. Now, in many public settings – political speeches, panel discussions, fundraising events—we are seeing increasing instances of Black women firmly and politely interrupting a speaker and offering them a chance to make a more truthful statement."

Dr. Robinson, thank you so much for sharing these incredible revelations with us about the effects of this mysterious pandemic. I'm sure you and your colleagues at the CDC will be keeping close tabs on further developments.

Let's turn now to my conversation with Ms. Estelle Davis. Ms. Davis is a third-grade teacher at PS 510 in Brooklyn, NY. I caught up with her after school last week and we took a stroll and reflected on her personal experience with this virus.

Ms. Davis, thank you for making time to talk with me. As a 3rd grade teacher, and a mom of three kids of your own, I'm sure you don't get much time to catch your breath.

"I really don't. Honestly, my days are usually a blur between getting my kids and myself out of the house in the morning, holding it all together through the school day, and then my husband and I juggling afternoon and evening activities to try to keep it all together. Actually, it was nice when your producers contacted me for this interview, it lets me take a moment out of my daily grind and think about all that has happened."

I'm sure it has been a lot. Tell us how this all started for you.

"Well, let's see. About a month and a half ago my whole classroom got hit by the new virus. First a couple of kids were sneezing, then a few more, and before you knew it, most of the children were home sick. Between my students and my own kids, I knew it was just a matter of time before I got it myself. But by then we were already hearing that the effects of the virus were relatively mild and there was no long-term danger. So, when I started my own sneezing fit, I stayed home and just let it pass and sure enough three days later I felt completely fine when I returned back to the classroom."

And so how did you come to find out that all was not normal.

"Yeah, that's the interesting thing for me. It actually took several days for me to notice."

Really? With such incredible new abilities, how could you not notice sooner?

"Well, the reality for me is that I have always been a steady person who tends to bring calm energy into the places where I am. I think it's the only way I've been able to keep teaching third grade in an underinvested inner-city public school for all these years."

Ah, so it wasn't that different when your classroom was calm around you and when your teachers' meetings were more orderly with you around.

"That's exactly right. I mean, after a while, it became obvious how sudden and complete the shift is when I am around. But at first, I thought it was just me being me."

How about the truth-telling?

"See, that's another one that kinda comes naturally to me. I've always been a deeply empathetic person, able to get a good read on people pretty quickly. My mom was the same way. And we kids could never get *anything* over on her. I'm like her, folks around me learn pretty quickly that I will call b.s. when I see it."

But eventually you realized that you were literally sensing the lies being told around you.

"Yup, for sure. Whereas before, it was just a light sense that something did not ring true, I realized that now it was clear and sharp in my mind, not only that I was hearing a lie, but also what the actual truth was. That was the new element to it."

I'm guessing, prior to the virus, you were not been able to heal people with your touch.

"Ha, oh that's for sure! I wish! Could have saved many a night in the ER with my little ones who have racked up too many injuries to count over the years."

So that's the new power that let you know something extraordinary had happened to you.

"You got it. I'll never forget my first healing. My class was at recess out on the playground. I don't know how Bakari got himself up to the top of the monkey bars and I didn't see him until he was on the ground, writhing and holding his poor broken arm. I rushed over to him and as I touched his shoulder to comfort him, the effect was almost instantaneous. He grew calm, he smiled at me, and you could just see his arm repairing itself. It was just unbelievable."

Wow. So what reactions have you experienced from others about your new powers?

"Hmm. Well, I guess I should not have been surprised. The initial reaction to us having these new powers was widespread fear and resentment. Folks just about lost their minds."

How so?

"Why had *we* been singled out for these new abilities? What would we *do* with these powers? White folks especially, they were very fearful of what this would mean for them. And, to be honest, Asians and Latinos and all the rest of them were the same way. Many just got scared and kept as far away from us as they could. At first, it was very isolating."

How sad.

"Yeah, even my own family. At first, my husband, sons, and brothers tripped out."

Really?

"Oh yeah. I mean, now it was truly no more gameplaying, no more trying to front. Just keep it real fellas. Don't *make* me call you out again! Yeah, at first this was extremely unsettling and for them."

But then?

"But then, I guess folks started to realize the universal benefits of these powers in my hands."

How so.

"Well, number one, the calming effect of my presence is key. Despite whatever fears and resentments someone holds in their minds about Black women and our new special powers, once they are in my presence they feel a sense of deep calm and comfort. I feel it too when I'm around another Black woman. You should be feeling it right now. It's quite soothing, isn't it?"

Oh my goodness, yes. And it feels very natural and gentle. Not like a calm that a pharmaceutical product might yield.

"I've talked with girlfriends of mine and we just love how much more chill things are at home. Not that there aren't still the usual tensions and disagreements – but when we walk into a room things just cool way down. And now wherever we are—the office, the grocery store, the coffee shop—folks just stop acting out unnecessarily. Even at the DMV and social security office, where there is always someone feeling some kinda way, folks conduct their business with courtesy and respect, and knuckleheads stop trying to jump the line."

Must be really nice.

"Our healing powers have become what folks really value. At first, we were just sought out when we were bystanders to a medical crisis in public. Boy, it was really something having people scan crowds eagerly, hoping to see one of us they could call on for our assistance.

Then our friends and other folks we knew personally, when they got hurt, began reaching out to us for a healing touch. Then eventually, hospitals and clinics and ambulances everywhere wanted to recruit some of us to be on their medical teams. Our power to heal injuries have made us invaluable as a part of crisis care teams."

And your truth-telling power. That has got to cause the most discomfort and avoidance around you.

"Whoo boy. The impact of our truthtelling power, now *that* was most fascinating. It didn't take long for folks to figure out that ain't no use lying when we were around, because we would just call you out in a second. C'mon, why you still out here lying?! So they stopped. Yup, stone cold stopped fabricating.

I can't tell you the number of times someone around me has started to tell a tall tale, looked right at me, cleared their throat, and just came correct with the real deal. And now, if one of us is present, conversations, speeches, and announcements become direct, accurate and to the point."

So I gotta ask you. How does all this feel? It must be an amazing feeling to have this power.

"Well....yes and no."

Oh really?

"Yeah. I mean, it feels great to have these abilities to influence things around me in such a positive way, for sure. And, like I said, some of this calming and truth-telling influence is something I already had. And the healing power is truly a blessing. But...it's also kind of a curse."

How so?

"Well, now there are all these expectations of me, of us, to be the super healers of society. I'm constantly getting called to the site of some kind of gruesome injury. And, yes, it's wonderful to be able to immediately do something about it. But, don't forget, I have to see all these people endure injuries and pain as well, *before* I heal them. Seeing all that suffering is taking a toll on me, I can feel it.

I may have these powers, but I am still very human. As a Black woman in America, I was already under tremendous strain to overcome everyday adversities while being the nurturer for so many others in my life. These powers have added to my burden, even though I feel more appreciated and empowered than ever before."

Ah. It's great to be needed and appreciated for your special powers, but at the same time the weight of this responsibility is a burden.

"Exactly."

Well, Ms. Davis, I know you need to get home to your family. Thank you for making time to take this walk with me and share your experience. Thank you for all you are doing to help others and I wish you the best in caring for yourself as you do it.

"You're welcome."

We turn now to my conversation with one of the leaders of the SistaPower Movement that has been formed to provide solidarity and support to Black women as they navigate the realities of their new powers and the opportunities and responsibilities that come with them. Ta'Layla Patrice is a member of the SistaPower Council and a local grassroots leader and activist in her hometown of Buffalo, NY.

I caught up with Ms. Patrice as she was preparing to head into a Council meeting.

Ms. Patrice, thank you so much for making some time to talk to us, I know your Council duties have you extremely busy.

"Yes they do, but this is an important opportunity to push back against the misinformation that is being shared about our efforts, so I'm willing to make a little time to talk."

Can you tell our audience about how the Council came to be, and what its role and function are.

"Sure. This is really all about how we should use the enhanced powers that we have."

I noticed you use the word "enhanced."

"Yes, that's vital. Many of you journalists are referring to these as new powers. But for many of us, maybe most of us, these are not new powers. We have been the peacemakers, the healers, the truth-tellers among you all for generations. But our powers have certainly been enhanced. And all of us now have all three of these abilities."

I appreciate your clarification. So the central question was how these enhanced powers should be used.

"Right. I mean, imagine these powers in the hands of White males? The first question would have been how to use the new powers to make money. Let's be real, that's what White guys would have done in a heartbeat. An Instant Healing Clinic Inc. on every corner."

Sounds like a fair point.

"And what about the discrimination and trauma we Black women have endured forever? Surely this was our chance for some vindication, some payback. Using our truth-telling power to truly shame some folks. Withholding our healing from those who had done us, or done somebody, wrong.

I'll keep it real. There were many of us who were inclined to use our powers to suit our own purposes, to advance personal interests and grievances. But, thank God, there were more of us who just wanted to set things right with our new abilities.

To finally make things right, once and for all.

Many of us who saw the chance for a brand new day, with we sistagirls setting the tone.

Most importantly, we had some amazing Black women leaders—in education, in politics, in business, in our houses of worship—who were so, so ready for this moment to set a new direction for society. And through our sororities, social clubs, and alumna networks we could quickly communicate and organize ourselves."

So how have those leaders guided a path forward?

"Over two hundred Black female leaders came together about a month ago at a special convening in Seneca Falls, NY."

Historically significant as the site where Sojourner Truth made her famed "Ain't I a Woman" speech at the first ever Women's Rights Convention in 1848.

"That's exactly right. We debated the pros and cons of our new powers and reached consensus that, if used for good, these powers could truly change the world.

For sure, some of the leaders argued that this was our reparations moment and we should not miss the opportunity to establish our own world domination. Why not use our powers to benefit those, and only those, who look like us?"

Yes, I wanted to ask you this. Why not use these powers for your turn to control world affairs?

"It was a beautiful deliberation to be a part of. Make no mistake, there was some serious debate and disagreement about how we should proceed. But ultimately, the all-encompassing calming power that we women leaders infused throughout our gathering was a critical factor in the emergence of a consensus that we should use our enhanced powers to promote *universal* benefit."

Amazing. So then what?

"We crafted the SistaPower Principles to guide how we would use our powers. We made a commitment that we would first and foremost establish processes for maintaining self-care, wellness, and solidarity among ourselves as we girded ourselves for our role as stewards of the new era. We formed the SistaHood Network to unite Black women behind these Principles and to provide support and solidarity with each other. Through our enhanced powers we can change this world, but not at the cost of our own humanity and well-being."

That's remarkable Ms. Patrice. How do you feel about how things have played out since that historic gathering in Seneca Falls?

"Well, after centuries of being marginalized and ignored and exploited, things are radically different. Now, across the country and across the world, everyone wants us African-American women in proximity. In their workplaces, in their neighborhoods, in their places of worship, suddenly we are being honored and welcomed and valued.

The world is coming to learn that we are the original nurturers. We have anchored our families, our neighborhoods, and our people. All the pain and suffering we have endured has hardened us, traumatized us, yes, but our journey has also made us more wise and resilient and determined.

It has been our capacity for love that has been civilization's glue through centuries of greed, hate, and oppression.

We have been the primary holders of radical love. Love of our children and all children. Love for our extended families. Love for our communities. Love for the best of what our oppressors could be, if ever a day of reckoning would come.

How much colder and crueler would the world be without Black women's capacity for love?

Healing. Calm. Truth. Our enhanced powers all grounded in the restorative capacity of love.

Now is our moment. This is our time."

Simply stunning, Sista Patrice. Thank you for your time and for your leadership. And above all, thank you to you and your fellow SistaCouncil leaders for your grace and magnanimity in this moment of reckoning.

Viewers, we have one additional conversation to close out our investigative reporting on this incredible pandemic and its aftermath.

Dr. Luz Ciffer is the former CEO of BioVax, Inc. I'll let him tell you about his personal epiphany himself.

Dr. Ciffer, thanks for your time. I understand you founded BioVax about ten years ago, and you've recently stepped down as CEO.

"That's correct."

Please tell us more about BioVax.

"We started BioVax in 2018 and were still in start-up mode when COVID-19 hit. We were among the early adopters of mRNA technology and we learned a lot during that period of accelerated experimentation. We were able to secure investments that enabled us to establish our own niche in the vaccine market."

I understand you were well-positioned to begin work on a vaccine against this latest pandemic.

"Yes, in fact, we were the first to decode the genetic sequencing of this virus and thus had a head start on creating a vaccine."

But then it turned out the effects for most people were even milder than the common cold, and a vaccine was unnecessary.

"That's right."

But you and your team at BioVax kept working to find a cure.

"Yes, we did."

Why?

"Because of the effects that the virus did have."

The new, I should say, the enhanced powers given to Black women.

"Yes. We, and some of our investors, believed that a cure was still needed for those effects."

Why Dr. Ciffer?

"Because we believed that no one should have those kind of powers. That it was a danger to humankind for a subset of the population to have such potential for control over others."

What about the healing power, surely that is a benefit to humanity?

"Sure, depending on who gets healed. But these women have the power to decide who gets healed and who does not."

My understanding is that there has not been a single instance of a Black women withholding healing from an injured person.

"Yeah, for now. But they could change their minds at any moment."

But how is that different from you producing a vaccine, and then decided who to sell it to, how much to sell it for, and whether to give some of it away?

"We have company protocols, and a board, and stakeholders, who oversee and influence such decisions."

Ah, I see. But you and your colleagues were particularly concerned about *who* had these new powers.

"Ummm, yes."

Please go on.

"Well...and I am not proud of this admission...because I am not a racist...nor were any of those of us working on this project...but..."

Yes?

"Well, we just felt concerned about all that power in the hands of Black women."

Why?

"Well, you know, number one, I mean, that's a lot of responsibility for one particular group of people."

I see. I wonder if you ever felt uncomfortable about all the power and responsibility in the hands of White males. But ok, and what else?

"Ummm, well there's all that anger and resentment they have about everything that's happened to them...Black Lives Matter and all that...and so we expected that there would be retribution against us."

Us?

"White people."

White people?

"Well, particularly White men."

Did BioVax have any Black women on the team?

"Ummm, no."

Any women?

"No."

I see. So you kept working on a vaccine. And then what happened?

"Everything changed."

Everything changed?

"Yes, everything changed. It became obvious that none of what we feared, what I feared, was coming to be. The healing effects. The calming effects. Even the truth-telling. It was all so...it was all so...good. And these women were acting...were leading with such grace and such integrity. I just...we just...didn't know it was possible."

Interesting.

"And then...and then it really hit home for me."

Oh, yes?

"Yes, my son was in a horrific car accident. There's no way he would have survived that. And he was saved and fully healed on the spot by a Black woman who, thankfully, was in the vicinity."

So that sealed it for you.

"That's right, I went straight to the lab that evening, deleted vital company files, and shut down the vaccine production lab."

Basically destroying millions of dollars of experiments and setting the process back to square one.

"Yes."

I understand you are now under investigation by the board of BioVax and it's likely you will face some severe penalties for your actions.

"That's right. But I've already been hearing from board members and other colleagues who are slowly coming around to my revelation.

The facts are clear all around us. This is not a threat. This is our chance to be better. All of us."

Thank you for your time Dr. Ciffer, and for your honesty.

That's our story for this evening viewers. What a transformative moment for humankind. We are all experiencing it together, and we will continue to bring you our latest reporting on the global effects of this unprecedented turn of events.

***

The Divinity

How satisfying to see humankind finally on a different path.

I just knew they had it in them. Why did it take me so long to recognize that Black woman held the key? Like the humans I have watched for generations, I vastly underestimated the transformative potential inherent in Black women.

Now, thanks to the daughters of a race of tenacious survivors, the power of love and mutuality over the power of greed and self-interest has been decisively demonstrated.

And the world will never be the same.

Author's Reflection

How to help readers grapple with the antiracist theme of restitution?

This was the task presented by this story. The discussion, advocacy, and action in the U.S. seeking restitution through reparations policy has been generally so limited and so episodic that I quickly determined I needed to reach beyond human agency to demonstrate a truly large-scale restitution, on the level of the racial harms for which reparations are morally and instrumentally justified.

I was also interested in writing a story with an omniscient first-person narrator voice, and this story became a good one to use the voice of God as an opening and closing. To move the heart of the story along, I decided to use a journalistic narrator/interviewer to set the context and then host the other voices that would give personal vantage points on what transpired. To truly center Black women, I wanted to make sure it was their voices that directly described how the restitution is experienced and navigated.

I had originally considered creating this entire volume of short stories in an Afrofuturist genre. As they took shape, most stories moved in other directions. The theme of racial restitution, given the human failure to achieve it, remained a good one to explore through a science fiction treatment or what Walidah Imarisha and Adrienne Maree Brown have termed "visionary fiction."

"Visionary fiction" is a term we developed to distinguish science fiction that has relevance toward building new, freer worlds from the mainstream strain of science fiction, which most often reinforces dominant narratives of power. Visionary fiction encompasses all of the fantastic, with the arc always bending toward justice. We believe this space is

vital for any process of decolonization, because the decolonization of the imagination is the most dangerous and subversive form there is: for it is where all other forms of decolonization are born. Once the imagination is unshackled, liberation is limitless.

Walidah Imarisha, Octavia's Brood: Science Fiction Stories from Social Justice Movements

The Queen of Afrofuturism is, of course, the magnificent Octavia Butler. This story is inspired by her pioneering afro-imagination and literary activism. Estelle was her middle name and Ms. Davis bears this name to honor her powerful legacy.

Using the voice of God to open and close the story invites readers to experience a particular conception of the Divine that may differ considerably from their own religious or spiritual understanding. This Divinity is an omnipotent creator that has provided free will to human beings and a deep capacity for love that we must discover on our own. This Divinity learns alongside humans as we fail over and over to elevate love over fear and greed. This Divinity, however, is not omniscient, and, like the rest of us, has overlooked and underestimated the capacities of Black women to help lead humanity to its best self.

This story is a love letter of appreciation to Black women. I wanted to center their very real powers, resilience, and grace which have all too often throughout world history been unseen, taken for granted, and, at worse, exploited and abused. My early versions of the story did too little to acknowledge the toll and emotional labor of having and deploying real or supernatural powers to support our families, workplaces, and communities toward a more just world.

As you consider the antiracist imperative of restitution, of making whole, of repairing past harms, who in your personal sphere of influence are you underestimated and devaluing?

What is your relationship to the Black women in your life, including yourself if you are one? Are there things you can change, in your mindset and in your actions, to be a part of restoring what has been taken or withheld from Black women?

Where could you make restitution by sharing and shifting power?

It's a Power Thing

President-elect Barack Obama had a massive decision to make.

He checked his watch. 3:15am. Saturday, December 1st. He slipped out of the bedroom quietly to avoid waking Michelle. He glided stealthily down the stairs in the dark, avoiding the creaky spots with a couple practiced lunges. He stepped out onto the back porch, eased into his favorite wicker chair, and stretched his lanky legs up onto the railing.

Although a winter chill was in the air, it was blessedly mild for December in Chicago and he'd be able to get in some precious moments of quiet rumination before having to head back inside to warm up. He reached behind the flowerpot and retrieved the pack of Marlboro Reds. He was really going to have to kick this habit once and for all now that the eyes of the Secret Service, not to mention the eyes of the nation, were going to be on his every move.

But not tonight.

A welcome calm settled over him as he took a first puff. Thank goodness Michelle had insisted that they have a quiet Thanksgiving weekend tucked away in their beloved home on the south side of Chicago for some final time as a family before things truly changed forever.

And then his brow furrowed as his mind began to enumerate the mounting list of political challenges to tackle. The task of forming his administration and designating key positions was the least of his worries – he had confidence in his transition team and knew that with the excitement and mandate of his election victory, they truly had the best and brightest at their disposal to recruit into government service.

More daunting was his elevation to power during wartime and the treacherous path ahead for U.S. involvement in Afghanistan.

Most daunting of all was the devastating reality of the rapidly spiraling global financial crisis. Those initial briefings had induced stomach cramps as he grasped the magnitude of the threat to the world economy that he and his team had inherited.

But none of these were first and foremost on his mind in these pre-dawn hours as he reached for a second cigarette.

Actually, he had awakened with a broad smile on his face and a glow in his heart reflecting on the incredible grass-roots mobilization that had thrust him to his historic campaign victory. They had done it. Yes. We. Can. Even he had been skeptical early on. Oh, he knew that they had to give it a try. The only possible way to vault a junior senator into the presidency would be to drastically shift the scope and breadth of voter engagement. And to draw campaign support from across typical lines of race and class.

From his voter registration experience fifteen years earlier with Project Vote! on the south side of Chicago, he knew that with the right tactics and ground game, people who had long tuned out of the political process, or had never tuned in, could be mobilized to engage. Many had dismissed him as young and idealistic, but he was determined to demonstrate that people who had been marginalized by the political process were eager to have their say, if given a chance. What a thrill it had been when ultimately 150,000 new African-American voters had registered to vote in the 1992 general election. We have awakened a slumbering constituency, he had said at time.

Just a few years later came his own march to elective victory to a State Senate seat. Though the veteran incumbent Bobby Rush had momentarily slowed his political rise with a humbling defeat in his bid for a congressional seat, that was now but a footnote to history. He had gone on to translate his grassroots mobilization prowess, and a particularly stirring speech at the 2004 Democratic convention, to galvanize support across rural and small-town Illinois and springboard himself into the U.S. Senate.

One of his favorite parts of the speech, which he believed had cut through the prevailing cynicism of the moment, was his appeal to the collective responsibility of the American people: ". . .it's not enough for just some of us to prosper. For alongside our famous individualism, there's another ingredient in the American saga. A belief that we are connected as one people. . .It's that fundamental belief - I am my brother's keeper, I am my sister's keeper - that makes this country work. It's what allows us to pursue our individual dreams, yet still come together as a single American family. 'E pluribus unum.' Out of many, one."

Just two years into his Senate term, the window had opened for his improbable bid for the U.S. presidency.

Seizing on the moment of disillusionment with the Republican party, and deploying ever more sophisticated mobilization tactics, he and his field team had hit the towns and farms of rural Iowa with a zeal and sense of possibility that was contagious. His upstart victory in the Iowa caucus gave notice to the world that his candidacy and electability were very real. His reference in his stump speeches to his belief in the fundamental decency of the American people may have seemed quaint and naïve, but it had been affirmed by thousands of face-to-face conversations across the country.

So now what?

The mandate was clear to govern the country toward the change he had compelling described.

But what about the grassroots movement that had galvanized behind his candidacy? What was next for the millions of Americans, of every race, class and even political affiliation, who had not only voted for him, but taken their time to knock on doors and make campaign phone calls? Many had volunteered for a political campaign for the very first time in their lives. He chuckled at the image of Chicago urbanites fanning out across the farms of Iowa.

His mind turned back to a conversation from the day before. He had huddled with his senior advisers at the transition team offices in Chicago to hear their recommendations about next steps with his base of campaign supporters.

"What an incredible gift you will give to yourself and the Democratic party to pivot your volunteers and donors into the most robust political support that any sitting president has enjoyed," said a seasoned adviser.

"I can't think of a president who has started his first term with such a wind at his back for his re-election," agreed another, "we play this right, and you can have these folks doing your bidding for the next four years."

"Whoa, whoa, whoa guys," the president-elect had declared with some annoyance, "let's not get ahead of ourselves here. First, I only want to hear talk about this term, not the next one. Second, I've been elected president, not king. We've got some serious thinking to do about what comes next for this coalition we've mobilized."

"What's there to think about?" the veteran adviser had queried. "We've got to move quickly to streamline as many of these supporters as possible directly into sustained financial and political support of your administration."

"We are sitting on thirteen million email addresses," another staffer stated, drawing out each word for emphasis. "Thirteen. Million. With the press of a button, those people all become members of your new personal political organization."

"We already have a name for it," added the campaign veteran. "Organizing for America. They've helped you get elected, now they can help you move your legislative agenda."

"My legislative agenda..." mused the president-elect, almost to himself. "Or *their* legislative agenda?"

There was a moment of confused silence in the room, as the senior campaign team looked at each other quizzically, trying to figure out if their boss was actually serious.

"There is another way."

All heads turned toward the new voice that had spoken up. It came from a young African American man who stood in the outer circle of staffers, ringed around the senior team. Ben James was known to all in the room as the most passionate field director on the team who had risen steadily in responsibility over the two years of the campaign. His round-the-clock energy was legendary, and his boyish charm and people skills had been invaluable in inspiring hundreds of volunteers to go way above and beyond their intended commitments. But he had never spoken out in opposition to the senior team.

Until now.

"Son, I'm afraid this conversation is well above your pay grade," one of the senior team members quickly countered, eliciting chuckles from some of the other staffers.

"Hold on," the president-elect interjected, holding up a finger to silence the team and beckoning Ben to continue with his other hand. "Let's hear him out. What's on your mind Ben?"

"Well," Ben started haltingly, as if his earlier pronouncement had made its way out of his mouth before his mind had a chance to intercept it. He was still getting used to this new reality that his community organizing journey had led him to this inner circle of political power. Who would have thought it? Sure, he had spent more time in high school rallying fellow students to support one cause or another than he had dedicated to his studies. And he had been voted "most likely to be a union leader." Selected to be the class speaker at graduation, he had been joined at the podium by the two young men he was mentoring through Big Brothers Big Sisters, and the three of them had shared their visions for a south side of Chicago that had all the vitality and opportunity of the city's affluent north side.

But he had hit a rocky patch after high school. His halfhearted attention to his studies had caught up with him and he had been waitlisted and then rejected from Morehouse College, the only college application he had submitted. The gap year he had taken while re-applying to Morehouse had been a pivotal experience. A family connection had secured him a staff intern position in State Senator Obama's office and he had been smitten by the poise, brilliance and infectious optimism of the young, rising politician. It had not taken much to convince him when, armed with his freshly-minted political science degree from Morehouse, the Obama US. Senate campaign had reached out with an offer of a staff position.

And now, here he was, staffing the transition team of the president-elect.

He exhaled and relaxed his broad shoulders, as if realizing that he might as well go all the way now that he had the room's attention, not to mention that of the next occupant of the Oval Office.

"We don't *have* to turn those folks into *our* political machine." As Ben spoke the words, the president-elect settled back into his chair with a grin broadening across his face, anticipating where the young field director was going with this.

"We can turn them into *their* own political machine."

Ben's boyish intensity began to emanate. His deep brown eyes sparkled as he looked around the room. "And not just a *political* machine. A *social change* machine. A grassroots change *movement*....for real. Not *just* to get someone elected, but to actually *change this country*."

He had gone too far. The room erupted in gasps and guffaws.

"*Just* get someone elected?!?" the veteran adviser sputtered as he sprang from his chair, "*Someone*?!?" His face grew red with anger. "Son, we have just won the most incredible political victory anyone has ever seen!"

Others jumped to their feet and crowded around Ben, the noise in the room swelled with multiple voices talking over each other. Finally, one of the senior staffers called a halt to the meeting and ushered everyone out of the room.

No one had noticed that the president-elect was still sitting pensively in his chair as they filed out of the room.

Now, as a faint hint of the approaching day began to glow in the sky, he stood decisively from the wicker chair and ground the cigarette out on the side of the flowerpot, then deftly covered it with dirt. He dialed a number on his phone and set up an impromptu morning meeting at his favorite breakfast spot.

***

Valois Cafeteria - See Your Food proclaimed the large sign above the entrance to the 53rd Street diner. Ben James loved this place. The sweet and savory smells enveloped him as he walked in—pancakes, waffles, sausages, bacon, coffee—along with the chatter of the clientele and the gruff voices of the cooks behind the transparent screens through which customers could watch their food being prepared as they ordered.

"Next! Whaddya want?" the lead cook demanded of Ben as he reached his turn at the counter. He placed his order and turned to take in more of the scene. Diners from seemingly every walk of life filled the tables around the large dining room.

At one table a group of older Black women conversed gracefully, he guessed they might be a book club. At another, a cluster of university graduate students of various races and ethnicities jabbered excitedly. Either a debate about Aristotle's philosophy of the good life or the visual effects of the recent Marvel movie, he surmised with a smile. Next to them a biracial couple gazed into each other's eyes as they chewed contentedly.

Ben allowed the scene to seep into his spirit. Maybe it *is* possible, he told himself. Maybe we *can* all get along. Given the right conditions, perhaps.

Having received his tray of food, he made his way over to the corner table for two where the president-elect had stationed himself, tactically positioned where his Secret Service agents could sit at the nearby tables, effectively blocking off a private space. This was Hyde Park, where sightings of Barack Obama were a regular occurrence and, besides the occasional tourist snapping a surreptitious photo, most of the other customers turned back to their meals after noting the president-elect's presence with obvious delight.

"Ben!" Obama smiled broadly as the young field director took a seat. The president-elect had already tucked into his meal of egg whites, turkey sausage, hash browns and wheat toast, far more healthy than most of the fare being consumed around the diner. He continued to eat as he eyed Ben warmly. "You sure got my team riled up last night."

"Sir, you really didn't have to take me out to breakfast personally in order to fire me," Ben's eyes expressed the appreciation that he felt, "I know you've got plenty of super important things on your to-do list."

"So," the president-elect interjected, "tell me more about this 'other way' of yours."

Ben froze. The piece of pancake drenched in syrup on his fork paused en route to his mouth. "Sir?"

"Yeah, giving the people their own organization. What's your vision for that?"

Ben took a moment to compose himself and his thoughts as he grasped the reality that rather than losing a job, he might be about to talk himself into one. A really big one. He delivered the bite of pancake to its intended destination, put down his fork and took a sip of piping hot coffee.

"Well sir, sure we could do what everyone would do, what your senior advisers want you to do, and turn that database of thirteen million supporters into a boring old political action committee. Keep your money coming! Write to your congressperson! Tell your neighbors to vote for my bill! The other guys are the bad guys!" There was that intensity mounting again. His eyes narrowed. "And sure, some of the supporters will stay with you, because that's all that they expect. And many will fritter away. Because that's all that *they* expect. Same old, same old. And they will all watch the thrill of campaign possibility become the grind of legislative wrangling."

He took another bite and chewed determinedly.

"Or we could shift the power to the people." Ben grinned as those words just felt so good coming off the tongue.

"Hand the database over to an independent organization. I mean completely independent. Not some Organizing for America that will magically become Obama for America in two years when you ramp up your re-election campaign." He leaned in closer to the president-elect. "Instead, you completely cut ties with the group. Unleash all that zeal for change into the neighborhoods and towns across America, unconstrained from the political manipulation your advisers are cooking up for it. And, believe me, most of your supporters will still be there to rally and vote for your agenda when you need them. But in the meantime, instead of waiting to be directed by *your* administration what to do, you will urge them, inspire them, to keep the momentum for change going right now, on whatever issues *they* deem important for their local communities."

Seeing that the president-elect was nodding approvingly, he pressed on.

"We've built a nationwide, multiracial coalition never before seen. But as soon as you hit that first legislative battle and begin to make inevitable tradeoffs, there will start to be fissures in our united front. Maintaining the current level of energy and solidarity using a centralized, political operation will be impossible. Without the narrow focus of a historic presidential election to galvanize folks, the coalition will peter out, I guarantee you."

The president-elect leaned back in his chair and stroked his chin, deep in thought.

The happy buzz of the diverse Valois clientele around them was the ideal setting for this pivotal moment.

"You've got six days," the president-elect finally stated solemnly. "Bring me a leadership team and a gameplan that will blow us all away."

***

Things proceeded quickly from there.

Ben's first move was a flight to Cleveland and a short drive to Oberlin College, the small liberal arts college renowned as a midwestern stronghold of the antislavery movement in the 1830s. He was here to recruit his first co-leader in the design of the new movement, the one person in America who he knew was primed for such a moment as this.

Professor Angela Michaels was nodding her head rhythmically to the pounding, hypnotic bass beat of some reggae dub music as she typed away at her laptop when Ben knocked on her office door. He had to knock again to get her attention. She looked up.

"Mad Professor!" he nodded approvingly, identifying the Guyanese-born musician and allowing himself a little sway in her doorway, grooving to the beat. The coincidence that he was indeed looking for a mad professor to join in this venture was not lost on him.

"You must be that insistent Obama campaign guy who called me yesterday," Angela responded, her eyes shining at his spontaneous dance moves, while her mouth pursed at being interrupted in the middle of her writing. "Brotherman, Sundays are my hideaway day to knock some stuff out, so this had better be *real* important."

Ben pulled up a chair. "You must be the only sister in America not excited to get a call from the Obama campaign these days," he said with a smile and a look of genuine admiration.

She flipped her laptop closed and fixed her chestnut eyes on him with a look that reminded him of his older sister chastising him for once again saying something goofy. "Please brother." She shook her head gently and sighed. "Look, I voted for your guy and all, and I wish all of y'all the best. But we've had our moment of euphoria, you all showed the world that White folks were actually ready to put a guy with the last name Obama into the White House, and now the wheels will begin to fall off the party bus."

"Oh yeah?" Ben responded, delighted to find that Dr. Michaels was even more dynamic in person than her prolific writing and dazzling speaking appearances had conveyed. She was academia's equivalent of a rock star. A political scientist with the wisdom of an ancient philosopher, the savvy of a community activist, and the heart of a social worker. At 35 years of age, she had already authored six books on democracy and civic engagement, the latest one awarded a Pulitzer Prize for her mesmerizing account of the abolitionist movement in America and its demonstration of the effectiveness of what she called highly distributed power. Most impressive to Ben were the Civics Slams she and her collaborators had created in public schools across America, combining civic curricula, gaming technology and community service to educate and excite youth about organizing around local issues in their communities.

"Yeah," she continued, "the right wing zealots are already sharpening their knives to begin undermining the legitimacy of our new president. He'll need to begin making tradeoffs and spending down his political capital immediately to address the financial crisis and the war in Afghanistan. I'm guessing he'll pick healthcare over immigration or gun control as his first major legislative priority and, like Afghanistan, many a crusading empire has been handed humbling defeat on those lands." Ben noted that she seemed confident yet wistful in her predictions.

"You guys will do what all politico robots before you have done and transform as many of those campaign donors and supporters as you can into your political minions, ready with cash and phone calls at the beck and call of his Majesty Barack."

Angela was taken aback when Ben burst out laughing at her last statement. "Whoo, that is something!" he chuckled, shaking his head, "that is *exactly* what those guys want to do. You called it Dr. Michaels!" He composed himself and pounded a fist on her mahogany desk.

"But that's not what's gonna happen."

"Excuse me?" she queried, refocusing her eyes on Ben as if she were only now really looking at him for the first time.

After he explained his mandate from the president-elect and their six-day window of opportunity, she canceled her plans for the week and hopped in his rental car to catch the next flight back to Chicago.

***

Their next stop was the Oakwood Shores mixed-income housing development on the south side of Chicago. They wound their way through lots with the old rundown red brick public housing that would one day be demolished, lots with gleaming new housing that included replacement units for public housing residents and units for high-paying newcomers to the community, and vacant lots that were caught in limbo between either stage. They pulled up in front of one of the new townhome units and Ben strode up to the front door and rang the bell.

A silver-haired woman with a deep brown complexion and a regal bearing opened the door. Her face broke into a smile when she saw Ben. "There's my favorite organizer!" she said, "now why did it take you so long to come back and see me?" Crystal Newsome was one of the most well-known and respected tenant leaders in Chicago. She had raised eight children in Ida B. Wells public housing, the development being demolished to make way for Oakwood Shores.

Though she held considerable influence throughout the housing estate, the neighborhood around it, and across the city, she had never held a formal leadership position and many times had declined nominations for election to the local advisory council. "Power corrupts," she would always say when her admirers would ask her why she would not take a formal position.

The new Oakwood Shores development had included some for-sale homes for public housing residents who were able to qualify for a special homeownership program and Crystal had proudly become one of those pioneers, achieving one of her life dreams of owning her home in her own community.

Crystal hustled Ben and Angela into her living room and insisted they each accept a slice of the sweet potato pie that she had just baked that afternoon. Framed photos of family members sat on every possible surface of her meticulously organized home and on every available wall space. Ben couldn't miss the one non-family member on display, a framed copy of his favorite Obama campaign poster with a stenciled portrait of the president in red, white and blue, and the word HOPE in large capital letters across the bottom.

"OK Ben honey, so now who is this sparkling young lady," Crystal asked, as they dug happily into their slices of pie, "and what brings you two a knockin' on my door?"

"Ms. Crystal, meet Dr. Angela Michaels," he pronounced, "the most brilliant democracy scholar east of the Mississippi." "*East* of the Mississippi?!" Angela couldn't resist taking the bait.

"I'm just messing around Ms. Crystal," Ben chuckled, "this lady is our top national scholar on democracy and you and I are going to help her put some of her theories into action."

"Oh we are, are we?" Crystal raised an eyebrow, "And why and how are we going to do that?"

"Why? Because your president asked you to," Ben stated simply, pointing a finger at the campaign poster.

Crystal's eyes narrowed and her gaze shifted from the framed poster back to Ben, with a new intensity.

"And how? Well, that's what the three of us need to figure out. But," he paused for effect and grinned, "we will have all the tech and networking capacity of the world's greatest political campaign at our disposal."

After Ben filled Crystal in on his presidential assignment and answered several of her questions, she stood up, folded her arms across her chest, and let out a big sigh. "Well, glory be," she marveled, "this is indeed quite a moment. Power to the people, huh. Well, let's see what we can cook up for my guy Barack." She headed out of the living room, calling over her shoulder, "y'all go unload your stuff from the car, I'll get your bedrooms ready."

"Wait, we're not staying here, Ms. Crystal, I wouldn't impose that on you," Ben protested.

She turned to face him, her eyes gleaming and her arms outstretched wide. "Honey, if we are going to shift power to the people, what better place to do it than right here where the people ain't never had no power?"

***

They formed an attractive trio as they strode into the large conference room in the transition team offices in the Chicago loop high-rise, five days later. Crystal entered the room first, resplendent in a bright orange dress that contrasted sharply with the grays and blues of the attire of the transition team staff already seated around the long conference table. Angela followed in a sharp, sensible pantsuit with a white collared shirt and a beaded necklace and bracelet in matching red, black and green. Ben walked in last. Given his familiarity with most of those in the room, and his identity as a community guy, he had dressed the most casually of the three, with dark blue jeans and a white polo shirt under a blue suit jacket.

The tenor in the room was deadly serious and Ben guessed that the team had likely been arguing about something highly contentious before the three of them had been summoned into the room. Imagine a debate about relinquishing political power being a mood lightener, he thought to himself.

The president-elect broke the ice by springing up from his chair and embracing Crystal warmly.

"And here's the lady no one can ever get to take an official leadership position," he announced brightly, "Ben you must have worked some real magic to get Ms. Crystal Newsome on your leadership team!"

"Mr. President, I mean, Mr. President-elect, are these folks making sure you are eating right, 'cause you are sure looking even more skinny than ever," Crystal declared, as she settled into one of the seats at the end of the table that were obviously intended for the presenters.

Obama next turned to Angela. "Very nice to see you again, Dr. Michaels," he said, shaking her hand as he leaned in for a polite kiss on her cheek. "Now, I would have anticipated you would also have kept your scholarly distance from the messy compromises of the political process. This is a true coup for us to benefit from your ideas. Ben, you've done wonders with your recruiting."

With this last statement, he reached out and shook Ben's hand firmly and then returned to his own seat at the head of the other end of the table and motioned for everyone to take a seat.

"Ok, let's get to it," his tone turned a bit more serious. "My next meeting is a briefing on climate change, so I'm hoping this conversation will be one of my more enjoyable of the day. What have you got for us Ben?"

Ben and his team had anticipated that the topics of the day would have been heavy and the mood in the room solemn and they had come prepared. He reached into his shoulder bag and pulled out several multi-colored spheres and rolled them on the table toward each of the seated attendees, including the president-elect. Intrigued smiles broke out on their faces as they received the spheres and picked them up.

"Rubik's cubes?" No surprise that the first to identify the spheres was one of the president-elect's nerdy senior economic advisers.

"I thought Rubik's cubes were square," the president-elect stated.

"Usually yes," Angela spoke for the first time, "but they eventually came up with a round one. If you twist them, you'll see that they work the same way as a regular Rubik's cube."

Sure enough, as those holding a sphere manipulated them in various directions, they could see that there were tiles of six colors on the spheres and the objective of the puzzle was still to regroup the mixed-up color tiles onto separate sides of a single color.

Angela continued, capitalizing on the group's curiosity about the spheres. "Imagine the sphere you are holding is the structure of the social movement we are proposing."

She held up one herself and asked: "Where is the leadership of this movement?"

She rotated the Rubik's Sphere in her hand.

She answered her own question as the transition team looked at her skeptically. "It's *everywhere*."

"Where is the entry point to this movement?"

Another rotation.

"It's *anywhere*."

"Where is the most power held in the movement?"

One more rotation.

"*Nowhere*."

She asked and answered the next question with greater emphasis.

"At which single point could you intervene to control the movement?"

"There *isn't* one."

Seeing that her demonstration had clearly landed on those around the table, she pressed on.

"And now, consider the colors. We have a multiplicity of colors on this sphere, but whether they are dispersed and integrated among each other," she held up a sphere with the colors scattered, "or aligned and gathered in their unique groups," with her other hand she held up a solved sphere with the colors each on their respective sides, "the structure and cohesion of the whole still holds. It can accommodate both diversity and affinity."

"Cute, very cute Dr. Michaels," one of the advisers piped up, tossing his sphere to a staffer standing behind him and crossing his arms. "I'm sure you'll now bring this into the real world for us, since the rest of America is not quite as orderly as your bucolic Oberlin campus."

"Happy to," Angela responded, "hang in there while we lay out the principles that will guide this movement, and then we'll explain how it would be rolled out in our real world." She turned to her brightly dressed co-leader, who was nodding her approval energetically. "Ms. Crystal?"

Crystal leaned forward, good and ready for her chance to address the room. "OK folks, there are three guiding principles to this thing. Real, real simple to say, but real hard to do."

"First principle: We *all* have power to make change – use it!" With the final phrase she jabbed her finger towards one of the advisers across the table.

"Second principle: Power is more effective when it is *collective* – share it!" Another finger jab at another adviser.

"Third principle: Change must be anchored *locally* – first focus your power where...you...are!" Three finger jabs with each of these last three words.

The president-elect nodded thoughtfully, "I recognize your theory of highly distributed power, Dr. Michaels, but I hadn't heard it broken down quite like this – I like your version Ms. Crystal!"

"Just keepin' it real, Mr. President. I'm sorry, I'm just gonna start calling you Mr. President now, Lord knows we ready for you," she declared. One of the advisers looked as if he were about to correct this deviation from protocol, but a slight shake of the president-elect's head stopped him.

Crystal continued, "If we're gonna truly make change, I mean really change how things work for those who have been left out, we gotta get the power closest to the action. I'm sorry Mr. President, you can't take this supporter power to Washington with you."

Sensing that the advisers were getting antsy, Ben jumped in. "And here's how it works."

He stood and strolled around the room as he laid out the gameplan.

"Rather than shutting down the local campaign offices, we transition them into *power transfer stations*."

"Very clever Ben," Obama noted, "I see what you did there."

"Thank you sir. My uncle is an electrical engineer, he'd like that one too."

He proceeded, "as you and your political team head to our nation's capital to run the country, your transition offices here in Chicago will be turned into an independent, short-term operational launch base. The launch base and the local power transfer stations will operate for one year, and one year only. Their task is to identify an existing local organization or network in each community that is well-positioned to serve as an ongoing hub for the local activity. In some communities it might be the YWCA, in others it might be a community development corporation, in others it might be a faith-based network."

Angela joined in from her seat. "The key is to build this with existing trusted organizations where we can, to save time and to leverage existing experience, networks and assets."

Now Crystal spoke up. "The priorities of this change movement would be determined by the people in each community. What issue is energizing folks there? What would keep busy, tired folks coming together for brainstorming? What would keep them knocking on their neighbors' doors? Local leaders will be encouraged to seize the momentum of all the engagement that this presidential campaign has generated to get to work on their most pressing local issues."

"And there's one more key thing," Angela added, "rotating leadership." She picked up a sphere again and twisted it dramatically. "We build a succession planning rotation into the leadership model from the very beginning."

"NO GATEKEEPERS!" Ms. Crystal bellowed, startling the advisers closest to her. "All groups will have co-leaders and all co-leaders will recruit future leaders to serve alongside them. When the co-leaders move on, they become resource leaders. Power can't corrupt if it is constantly flowin'."

Ben wrapped up their initial pitch. "We know that in many, perhaps most locations, there will not be the organizational capacity to manage a movement hub in the early days. But if even one out of every twenty campaign offices can get a hub off the ground, we can use those as pilot sites for the first couple years and then expand from there."

Ben passed around thin spiral-bound copies of their proposed movement strategy. The assembled advisers flipped through the document and began to pepper the threesome with detailed questions. For forty-five minutes the lively conversation flowed back and forth, as Ben and his team patiently and deftly managed the critiques and concerns raised by the group.

With his approving smile and relaxed demeanor, it was now abundantly clear to all that the president-elect had already been thinking along these lines himself, and the vision, mission and principles of this proposition resonated deeply with his own community organizing philosophy. Maybe such a change effort would indeed keep local engagement high and serve as a base for future campaigns. So after failing to undermine the idea, the advisers shifted to offering constructive criticism and some specific suggestions for how to set it in motion.

Finally, the president-elect stood, and strode over to look out the 12th floor window as if imagining the hubs actively organizing in the

Chicago west side neighborhoods that stretched as far as the eye could see. He echoed the guiding principles back to them.

"Use *your* power."

"*Share* your power."

"First focus your power *where you are.*"

He smiled.

"Very catchy. And what do we call this movement?"

The three co-leaders looked at each other, beamed, and responded in unison.

"OurTurn."

***

The OurTurn movement hit numerous snags, but ultimately proved to have some sustained impact, particularly in communities that had a local organization that was primed and ready to serve as the local hub. As expected, only about a third of the seven hundred Obama campaign field offices were able to stand up a self-managing hub within the allotted time period. But this still meant over two hundred new movement hubs across the country. And Ben and his team stayed true to the power shifting plan, which confounded the naysayers who accused the Obama administration of a devious scheme to skirt campaign finance rules. The transition launch base and the power transfer stations were shut down after a year and the local OurTurn hubs were left to forge their own paths forward, with technical assistance from a network of consultants funded by national foundations.

The local movements were invariably driven by a few highly committed community members, including some who had not been civically engaged prior to the Obama campaign, and thus had lots of energy and optimism about making things happen. The OurTurn hubs focused on a wide array of topics—public education, teen mental health, crime and safety, community walkability, senior care, environmental justice—the commonality being a pressing local need or moment of opportunity. The most impactful hubs were able to use the central launch base and technical assistance to connect with regional or national government or nonprofit efforts that had resources to address the selected issue.

The movement faced its most precarious moment about three years into the effort with the confluence of two factors. Obama's re-election campaign was getting off to a slow start and some of his advisers were ramping up pressure on him to more formally activate the local movement hubs to take on fundraising and political outreach. Concurrently, some of the OurTurn hubs had taken on a strident anti-war focus and were criticizing the president for his much greater use of drone strikes than his predecessor.

But by now the president had become a big fan of the OurTurn movement. He loved seeing the statistics on the rise of civic engagement in neighborhoods and towns across America and on the decrease in factors like voter apathy and social isolation. His healthcare legislation had passed far less narrowly than expected, in part because the local town halls that his political opponents had set up to lambast the proposed legislation were often flooded by OurTurn members, across party lines, clamoring with their neighbors for common sense health care reform. This had enabled him to pivot to a focus on immigration reform sooner than expected, which promised to provide a boost to the economy and to deprive his future opponents of a hot button issue to criticize him about.

Maybe one of his biggest legacies as president would be something he did *not* lead himself.

It was the people's turn.

Author's Reflection

This short story is dedicated to the memory and everlasting activist spirit of my big brother Ben Butler, who mentored me into the community development world over thirty years ago. Ben's father's middle name was James as is Ben's son's, and it was an honor and a thrill to bring Ben James to life infused with the spirit, instincts and zeal of my friend Ben, and see what a young visionary community network builder in the Obama inner circle would have done at that critical moment in recent history.

Readers who have read *Doing It Our Way* have already been introduced to the powerful techniques of community network building and the work of Bill Traynor and Frankie Blackburn and their organization Trusted Space Partners. Once again, I have used this didactic fictional space to channel their insights and provide a very practical how-to demonstration of an alternative community network building path to transformative change.

Some readers will recognize the real-life academic rock star philosopher Dr. Danielle Allen of Harvard University in the character of Angela Michaels. I was a post-doctoral scholar at the University of Chicago when Danielle was beginning her meteoric career there and I got to experience her mesmerizing intellect in person. I've watched with deep admiration as she has continued to advance the theory and practice of justice and democracy, including a recent run for governor of Massachusetts.

The character of Crystal Newsome is also near and dear to my heart, based on two grassroots Chicago leaders whose wisdom and savvy have been a key part of my learning journey. Shirley Newsome was a long-time resident leader in the south side neighborhood of

North Kenwood-Oakland whose style was one of graceful determination and consensus-building. Crystal Palmer, now leading tenant advocacy at the Chicago Housing Authority, was a public housing leader whose fierce advocacy fueled a legal consent decree that ensured resident oversight of the design and execution of mixed-income transformation at the Henry Horner Homes development on the near west side of the city.

This story is also a love letter to the remarkable grassroots organizing movement that my friend Barack and his team built to propel a young idealistic-pragmatist community organizer into his historic presidency. My wife and I were blessed to form a friendship with Barack and Michelle prior to his first foray into politics, that was then deepened as we each became first-time parents within two weeks of each other back in the summer of 1998. She and I chuckle now at the memory of being on his very first policy committee during his run for State Senate in Illinois. I remember being so proud of his positive reaction to the policy brief that I wrote for him about the pros and cons of a third airport for the Chicago region. That was oh so long ago. I remember distinctly a lunch with Michelle in the University of Chicago Hospitals cafeteria when she told me about Barack's plans to run for U.S. Senate and stated firmly that this was the final run at higher elected office she was going to allow before she would insist that he settle down and get a regular job that would deploy his talents in a way that could bring stability to their young family. Well, history sure swept the First Black Family forward after that!

The question of what to do with the grassroots movement as President Obama took office was one to which I gave a lot of thought at the time. Not having any influence in his circle of advisers, I watched from my perch in the cheap seats, hoping that he would unleash the movement as its own independent force, rather than turning it into a conventional political action committee. There is a draft somewhere in a digital archive of an op-ed piece co-authored with my friend David White in December 2008 making our case to the president-elect. We lacked the access and courage of Ben James to follow through on speaking up.

This story explores the what-if, the path not taken.

And hopefully it can inspire your thinking about an alternative path to change-making at the local level.

"It's a Power Thing" was the slogan of the young Barack Obama's successful voter registration drive in 1992.

How might you apply more creative, inclusive network-building techniques to advance progress on the issues that you care most about?

When, in a future meeting, might you raise *your* hand and say "there is another way..."

Afterword

I hope these stories have deepened your understanding of antiracism and equipped you with practical approaches you can apply daily in your various spheres of influence: self, family, peers, neighborhood, workplace, civic life.

Above all, I hope the ideas and revelations here have inspired you to elevate your own antiracist commitment.

May you be a lifelong learner about the realities of race and racism in America.

May you be a discerning disrupter of systemic forms of racism.

May you confront and transcend your own implicit biases.

May you promote belonging and reduce othering.

May you name historical and current truths and counter myths and avoidance.

May you cultivate healing from racial harms, in yourself and in others.

May you help make whole those who have been wronged.

May you have the courage to share and shift power to the vulnerable.

Acknowledgements

O ne of the joys of writing this volume of short stories was the support and encouragement I received from so many friends and colleagues.

From their incisive feedback on the first draft story that I shared with them, I learned that my former students and employees, Emily Miller and Sherise McKinney, are fellow literature aficionados with a sharp editorial eye and a great feel for tone and story structure. They agreed to take on a more formal role editing the story drafts and this final version is tighter and truer thanks to them.

I benefitted greatly, in motivation and momentum, from a small, dedicated group of friendly reviewers who eagerly read and responded to my story drafts as soon as I shared them. Many thanks to Braveheart Gillani, Andrew Richman, John Lentz, Quentin Smith, Frankie Blackburn, Debbie Wilber, Alyssa Nickell, and Nancy Rolock for reading and giving feedback on all eight stories. But most of all, thanks for your genuine enthusiasm about what I was producing.

The first five stories were written during a brief academic sabbatical in the summer of 2023. To get time away from our daily routine, my wife Me'lani and I headed to California and sojourned from Los Angeles to the Bay Area with a series of stays with friends and family. Our gracious hosts left me alone to write for much of the day and then socialize in the evenings. My gratitude to Carlos and Gloria Velarde,

David White and Lorenza Munoz, Akeem and Tracy Ayeni, Vera Labat and George Spencer, and our gracious AirBNB host in the Napa Valley.

Concurrently to writing these stories, I have co-developed a new graduate course centered around my Everyday Antiracism framework. A shout out to my wonderful co-designers and co-instructors Dr. Jennifer King and Dr. Braveheart Gillani. We have included the stories among the readings for the course. Thus, the almost ninety students who have now taken Operationalizing Antiracism for Everyday Impact have served as fabulous early commentators on the story drafts. It has been gratifying to listen in on their small group discussions of the stories and to hear them reflect together on the insights and lessons that I hoped they would find therein.

Shout out also to longtime collaborator and friend Joni Kaden who is now partnering with me to help coordinate my Everyday Antiracism speaking and coaching practice. One of her many talents is graphic design. Along with managing production design for the volume, she created the cover design and helped produce the Everyday Antiracism visual that appears in the first few pages and at the start of every story.

I am also deeply grateful to family members who made time to read and comment on the stories. My uncle Michael Joseph was one of those readers who seemed to consume the stories and send back reactions as quickly as I could write and share them. My mother, Jennifer Joseph, offered both pride and encouragement as well as some of my sharpest critiques and questioning.

There were many sources of inspiration for the stories in this volume and I credit many of them in the Author's Note after each story. There are a couple of people whose influence spans the entire volume. Theo Miller, a social change agent par excellence, was the architect of the five-year phase of the HOPE SF mixed-income redevelopment in

San Francisco that he framed as a "reparations initiative." His conception of the importance of truth, healing, and restitution in racial justice greatly influenced my Everyday Antiracism framework. Dr. Amy Khare, a colleague and comrade for over twenty years now, was the Research Director for our seven-year mixed-income research study in Chicago and then a collaborator in numerous ventures since then. She led our first scholarly paper that foregrounded the issue of race and has continued to influence and inspire me with her commitment to personal and social truths, as uncomfortable as they may be to name and confront.

One gift of this writing endeavor is a reconnection and new phase of friendship with the renowned author Sarah Ladipo Manyika. I became lifelong friends with her husband James while we were both studying at Oxford University over 35 years ago. I met Sarah back then and have kept in light touch with James over the years. A recent reconnection with both of them led to Sarah agreeing to review and offer suggestions on my draft manuscript. You can imagine the validation that her affirming feedback and encouragement gave me, at a critical juncture in moving the book to publication. Her gentle critiques and line edits have enhanced the stories and identified key ways I can grow and improve my writing in the years to come.

I am blessed with three adult children who each made time to review some of their crazy dad's creative endeavor in the midst of their busy Gen Z lives. Our youngest son Ayande read the most stories and offered wonderful feedback and validation. Our middle child Malik expressed the most avid enthusiasm about my writing journey and shared high appreciation of the stories he read. Like her grandmother, our daughter Layla offered the strongest critiques and, as I note in the volume, inspired a major rethinking of the Restitution story (which was wisely anticipated by her brother Ayande who asked after reading it, "have you gotten feedback from any Black women yet?").

Finally, my best friend and fellow life adventurer, Me'lani Labat Joseph, has always offered loving affirmation of my "way with words," and expressed confidence and belief in this writing quest from the beginning. She supported my hunkering away during that summer sabbatical trip and the Thanksgiving and Christmas vacation that followed and continues to be a wonderful accountability partner as we each continue to seek ways to make positive change in our world.

About the Author

Mark L. Joseph, Ph.D., is the Leona Bevis and Marguerite Haynam Professor of Community Development at the Jack, Joseph and Morton Mandel School of Applied Social Sciences at Case Western Reserve University. He is the Founding Director of NP3: Nurturing People. Power. Place., formerly the National Initiative on Mixed-Income Communities. Joseph is an influential speaker, coach and consultant with a cutting-edge approach to advancing racial equity and justice through Everyday Antiracism. He is a graduate of Harvard University and the University of Chicago and was a Harlech Scholar at Oxford University. He is the co-author of the award-winning Integrating the Inner City: The Promise and Perils of Mixed-Income Public Housing Transformation along with numerous publications on urban equity and inclusion. Joseph draws from over thirty years of research and practice in community and social change to promote personal, organizational and community transformation. He and his wife live in Cleveland, Ohio and have three adult children.

Mark is available for book clubs, keynotes, workshops and coaching engagements.

More information at www.everyday-antiracism.com.